HOME STRANGE HOME

CEECEE JAMES

For my Auntie Lala and Auntie Lili, who extolled the values of laughter, a good story, and broccoli.

CONTENTS

Blurb   vii

Chapter 1   1
Chapter 2   16
Chapter 3   29
Chapter 4   41
Chapter 5   53
Chapter 6   60
Chapter 7   66
Chapter 8   78
Chapter 9   92
Chapter 10   100
Chapter 11   108
Chapter 12   115
Chapter 13   122
Chapter 14   134
Chapter 15   144
Chapter 16   150
Chapter 17   159
Chapter 18   168
Chapter 19   177
Chapter 20   186
Chapter 21   197
Chapter 22   208
Chapter 23   216
Chapter 24   224
Chapter 25   229
Chapter 26   237

BLURB

When Stella's uncle drags her to a surprise party for Ian Stuber, no one is more surprised than the man of the hour--who promptly drops dead. But when it's determined something more sinister is at play, Stella is dragged into the investigation as one of the witnesses, and the search is on to discover not only WHO committed the murder, but HOW... after all, the room was packed with party goers.

Sniffing out a killer is a hard enough task by itself, but when you add to the fact Stella's own family keeps stonewalling her every move to search for her missing mother, it's no wonder Stella is about to lose her mind. She's soon learning that if she wants answers, she's going to have to find them herself.

Can Stella capture Ian's killer before he strikes again?Or will the next bullet be for her?

---

*Y*ou know that tickley sensation of sweat gathering in places where it absolutely shouldn't be, and you're trapped in public, unable to do anything about it? Like a spider snared in my shirt, the prickle was a red bullseye of misery, becoming all I could think about. I squirmed, unfortunately knocking Darrel in his spine.

"Ow!" he said, pushing back into me. My nose bumped into the sofa.

It's not what you're thinking. I was actually hiding behind a sofa, along with five other people, on this grand Saturday afternoon. Unfortunately, the sofa wasn't big enough to hide six grown adults, and so we were stacked on top of each other much in the same way as ingredients on a sub sandwich. I was the tomato, being squashed in both directions.

The room was sweltering, and the surrounding air was heavy with the scent of sweat and halitosis. I tried to breathe through my mouth. Someone coughed, and the whole stack of us wobbled as we fought to balance against each other. I won't even tell you where I found a spare elbow.

We were waiting for my Uncle Chris's long-time friend to show up. Ian Stuber was his name, and he was about to leave our little Pennsylvania town of Brookfield to make his fortunes in New York City. This was a surprise party, set up by my uncle to wish both him and his wife good luck on their new adventures.

"Quiet, everyone! He's here!" whispered a blonde woman with short hair. The nervous giggles increased as our human pyramid threatened to spill out onto the floor.

"Shhh," we warned each other.

Silence fell as the metallic scratch of a key against a lock came from the front door, followed by the sound of the door banging open against the stop. Footsteps clicked against the tile entry way, along with the sound of him taking off his coat.

The tower of us practically vibrated in anticipation. Almost here... just a few more steps....

As if we were one animal, I could feel the tension in all of us building in readiness to explode with shouts of "Surprise!"

Suddenly, from the entryway, Ian yelled, "You can't do this to me! That's extortion!"

His voice immediately put a damper on our excitement, like rain on a campfire. We eyeballed each other, wondering what we should do now. No one made the first move.

"If you do that, I swear I'll kill you!" Ian growled, stomping into the living room.

I glanced over at Uncle Chris, who had earlier somehow managed to squeeze his great girth behind a wing chair. His eyes were wide, his cheeks red and puffed as if he were holding his breath. He must have felt me looking at him because he turned his head to meet my eye. Then, slowly, he grabbed the back of the chair and climbed to his feet.

"Surprise," he called weakly, spurring us all to rise to echo the same sentiment. It was a weak celebration, I'll tell you that.

Ian's head swiveled in our direction so fast I thought his neck would snap. His jaw opened slackly, and his face drained to the color of congealed oatmeal. One of his hands slowly dropped to his side.

I can honestly say, in all my years of attending surprise parties, I'd never seen a person more surprised than him.

He swallowed hard and then smiled, the kind of smile you give your dentist when he's telling a joke but he's also approaching your mouth with a drill.

"I'll call you back," he snapped into his phone and then turned it off. His gaze rested on Uncle Chris. "Chris! Dude! How'd you get in here?"

Uncle Chris's sheepishly grinned and straightened his shirt. Even dressed casually, he wore a button-up. He wiped his forehead of sweat. It was hot in here, but I could tell he was sweating for other reasons. "Your wife let us in. We're all here to celebrate your move and the new job."

Ian's facial expression did a one-eighty. His head tipped back and he laughed. He even slapped his knee. "You guys got me! What is this, prank Ian day?" He pointed his phone at us. "Just got off the phone with my brother, trying to kid around about me not going to mom's birthday this weekend. He was planning on telling them I was headed to St. Johns instead. "

It was a curious explanation, but one we accepted with relief. Laughter trickled through the air as he stuffed the phone in his pocket. "So, a party, huh? After all that, you guys better bring it. Let's party!" he announced.

We all spread out while Ian went around the room, welcoming each of us. He smiled genially and waved our

4

congrats away, rubbing his other hand against his balding brown head in a show of humbleness.

I fanned my shirt for a breath of air. I hated crowds. I hated parties where I knew next to no one even more, but Uncle Chris had insisted. He'd put great effort into inviting everyone he could think of. There were people that they'd graduated college with, guys that they'd competed in car races with, and men from their personal business. Kari had even come, lugging a huge pot of homemade potato salad. She hadn't heard the event was catered and thought it was a pot-luck.

Jasmine, his gorgeous, young wife, tossed back white-blonde curls from her shoulder and sauntered up to Ian. "Surprise, baby," she said, before giving him a big kiss. When she finished, she carefully wiped the lipstick from his bottom lip with her thumb. "You happy?"

He grinned and winked. "Very. But I owe you one."

Standing next to Jasmine was the first blonde woman, the one who'd announced that he had arrived. She was so close, it looked like she was about to kiss Ian, too.

"Who are they?" I asked Kari.

She glanced at them and then back at me. Her lips raised in a small amused smile. "That's Jasmine and her cousin, Celeste. They're best friends, or so I've heard."

Jasmine and Celeste were such a fascinating pair that it was hard to drag my eyes away. The two appeared almost like twins, with skin as pale as milk, and the same silky platinum-blonde hair. I'd honestly never seen hair color in that exact shade before, outside of my childhood Malibu Barbie. Both young women were thin and well dressed in the latest designer clothes, with the cunning tears and rips in the jeans to make them appear bohemian even though they cost more than what I earned in a month.

Celeste stood tall in knee-high boots and pouted as her finger ran under a very expensive necklace. She muttered to Jasmine and rolled her eyes. Jasmine stepped back from Ian and nodded.

"The one with the short hair sure doesn't look like she's having any fun," I whispered to Kari.

"I don't think anything, outside of a nightclub filled with A-listers would interest Celeste very much." Kari casually examined her nails, making a show of not looking. "There are rumors that she's an escort of a certain kind."

"Ohh," I said, raising my eyebrows knowingly, even though I had zero idea what she meant.

"You know, the kind that accompanies the very rich in their yachts overseas. So yes, I'm sure Celeste has seen and met everyone I could only hope to see with a twelve dollar movie ticket."

"Well, that's nice that she made time to come to Ian's surprise party."

"Yeah." Her brow puckered. "Odd."

Now that she mentioned it, it did seem odd. And the young, blonde woman didn't look happy about her decision.

After about a half hour more of mingling, the catering staff gathered us to the table. The party was billed as a barbecue, and the smokey scent of ribs, brisket and sausage made my stomach growl.

I was a little intimidated when I arrived at my seat. On my right was Celeste, appearing like an ice-princess. A man in a tweed suit was on my left. I stared longingly at the end where Uncle Chris sat, laughing uproariously at something Ian had said. I watched him, remembering the strange text he'd sent me the other night. In it, he'd said that he needed to tell me about something, and he hoped I wouldn't hate him after I heard. My brow wrinkled now at the thought.

"My name's Celeste," the woman introduced herself, interrupting me from my reverie.

I was surprised and happy that she took the initiative. Maybe this wouldn't be as bad as I thought. "Stella."

"Stella," she rolled my name in her mouth as if tasting it. "How lovely and unusual. And how do you know our wonderful guest of honor?" She glanced conspiratorially at Ian.

"My Uncle Chris is good friends with him. He's also helping Ian sell this place. Flamingo Realty."

"I see. That explains the flamingo sign out front. Actually, that explains so much." She nodded, glancing around the table at the other guests. The waiters were passing out plates. "This is quite a good turnout."

"For sure," I agreed. It was true. The dining room table was huge, and every seat was filled with what appeared to be happy people. The wine was flowing, and the conversation was easy going around the table.

"So, how do you know Ian?" I asked, even though I knew. It wouldn't do very well to blab that she'd already been the subject of party gossip.

"I'm Jasmine's cousin. Her family lived in our grandparents' house when her father inherited the estate after they had passed. My father was not included in the will, and for a good reason. Jasmine took care of me though, during those tough years." She glanced at her cousin. Jasmine was leaning toward Ian and speaking softly. "And I suppose, I've taken care of her. She's needed me to stand up for her from time to time.

She's a peach. Sweet, and also soft. She's always been prone to bullying. So, it was hard on her when I left for college." Celeste concluded. She sipped her wine. Her sips turned into gulps and, in two seconds, it was half gone.

"But she's made it now." I smiled, trying to wiggle out of her verbal quicksand of family drama.

"If you can call being married to him, 'making it,'" Her gaze shot icy daggers in his direction. "He's never home, leaving her here alone night after night."

I was now up to my eyeballs in this sticky situation. Valiantly, I made another effort to steer the conversation. "So you went to college then. What did you study?"

"Studies? That's not always the important part, is it? The studies? Sometimes it's more about the escape," she answered. Her eyes focused on me like two blue lasers.

The way she said the word 'escape' made my blood run cold. I wiped my mouth with a napkin to stall for time, trying not to react. Finally, I answered, "I'm sorry there were things in your life that you felt you had to escape."

Her eyes continued to study me, sharp and knowing. "Escape, evolve, and change. I travel the world now. They say the best revenge is a life well lived."

I nodded. "I've heard that saying before. It's very true."

"At any rate, I am here now, living life at large. And forever thankful to our little Jasmine."

A rattle of silverware commanded our attention to the front of the table. Ian had thrown down his utensil and turned to glare at Jasmine. She appeared frightened.

Uncle Chris nudged Ian's arm.

"Calm down. Smile. It's a party," Uncle Chris encouraged. And then he seemed to try to change the subject by saying, "Now tell me how I'm going to finish my bid for Brookfield Mayor?"

Ian unclenched his hand gripping the cloth napkin. He forcefully relaxed his face and turned his attention to Uncle Chris. Soon they were talking animatedly about political campaigns.

Celeste hummed next to me. "It's a pity none of his family could be here to help celebrate. Or, perhaps, no wonder, with that temper of his."

"None?" I asked.

"His brother doesn't seem to have been able to make it. And his parents are gone."

A waiter set a plate brimming with barbecue before me. I thanked him and then turned to Celeste. "I thought he said his brother threatened to tell his mom he couldn't come to a birthday party?"

She picked up her fork. "Oh, that's his foster mom. His birth parents died in a car accident when he was a young boy. Although, I do believe they're here in spirit. At least his mother." She raised a blonde white eyebrow. "Literally."

"Literally?" Goosebumps rose on my arms, and I self-consciously rubbed at them.

"Oh yes, the Stubers are known for haunting their descendants. And with it being Ian's mom, I'm sure she's very close. They're in the shadows. Always watching." She shrugged a thin shoulder. "You know how mothers are."

I must have reacted because her sharp gaze zeroed in on me, again. "Are you close to your mom?" She speared a bit of salad.

And, just like a wet fish flopping on the end of a line, there it was: the question I'd skirted around my entire life. My mom.

Growing up in Seattle, people were used to the idea that my mother wasn't around. It had been commonly accepted throughout my school years that it was just Dad and myself. Of course, every now and then, someone would ask about her, but I'd always managed to fend off any curiosity with a casual, "Oh, she's been out of the picture since I was little."

I cleared my throat now in preparation to deliver the party line. "I don't know my mom. It's always been just my dad and me."

Celeste's eyebrow flickered slightly at my answer. "I see. So, did your parents divorce, then?"

Of course, that was the reason I always gave. But, as I opened my mouth to drop the yes, I paused.

Why *did* I believe that my parents had divorced? My mind raced through childhood memories until one surfaced of my dad explaining to me that I needed to use that excuse with my first-grade teacher. He'd told me that the word meant two parents weren't together anymore. And I'd blindly accepted it.

A chill ran down my neck. Was that what really happened? Had my parents been divorced?

I swallowed as my inner voice poked with another question. *Were they ever really married?*

The enormity of that thought caused me to gasp. "I don't know," I finally stuttered. "My dad mentioned something like that, but we've never really talked about it. I was a child. It was what he'd had me tell my teacher."

"How young were you when he said that?" she asked, her expression softening.

"Oh, about six," I answered, remembering that day. I'd worn light-up sandals with pink embroidered flowers. I'd loved those things, and been more concerned about stomping my feet to get the shoes to light up than in understanding the complicated word my father was sharing.

"And you've never seen her since?"

I shook my head.

Celeste leaned back in her chair. "There were no talks of visitation? No custody issues?"

"We never really talked of her again." I rubbed my neck, still creeping with chills.

"That seems highly unusual, don't you think? You don't suppose it's possible he's kept you from her, do you?"

What had I thought? No, I thought my mother had wanted nothing to do with us. The way my dad had cried when my mother had left... he'd been heartbroken.

I shook my head, my arms crossed. My father was a good man. He'd never do something as low as kidnap me. "It destroyed him when she left. I think she was done with us. She broke his heart. In fact, he's never even dated again."

"Hmm." Her brow puckered, and she tapped her lip. "Very peculiar."

"It's just normal life for me."

Her eyes widened. "You don't suppose, being that you were so very small, that your mom died, do you? Perhaps your father never knew how to tell you. He just said she went away. That happens, you know."

I picked up a fork. To be honest, I was trying to stall, desperate to do anything I could so that I could catch my breath. This woman was mentally sharper than me, and there was no knowing what she'd say next. Her words felt like a deluge of water pouring over me. I set down the utensil and fanned my face.

"You okay?" she asked.

At that moment, a man and a woman peered in through the dining room doorway.

"Knock! Knock!" said a heavy-set dark-haired man with a grin. He waggled a bottle of wine. "I heard someone was having a party!"

"Gordon Taylor!" shouted Ian from the head of the table. He stood, and they shook hands.

"Please! Have a drink," shouted Gordon. He popped the cork to the squeals of some of the women. Ian looked at his glass confused. It still had an inch of wine in it. He quickly drained the glass and then held it out.

Gordon filled it up.

Jasmine covered her glass with her hand. "Sorry, I'm not drinking."

"Oh come on. This is the good stuff!" Gordon said. He turned the bottle so the label could be read. I had no idea what it was, but several of the guests let out impressed sighs.

Ian sipped it and wrinkled his nose. Finally, he nodded. "It's good. Very good. Please! Have a seat."

The caterer brought over a few more chairs. We all scooted down, chairs rumbling against the floor, until there was a sliver of space available for the new guests.

I turned toward them, welcoming the distraction. Welcoming it so hard that I would have taken anything at that point to stop the conversation between Celeste and me.

Little did I know what was coming next.

2

After the neighbors had finally settled into their seat, things got back to normal around the table. Celeste turned toward me, her chest rising as she drew in a breath. By the pursing of her lips and the raised eyebrows, I imagined she wanted to pop off another round of questions. Rapidly, I spun toward my other neighbor.

"Are you enjoying the food?" I asked the man, my voice high and filled with desperation.

The man appeared to be in his fifties, with wrinkles just starting to whisk out from around his eyes and mouth. His pasty-white skin color accentuated the enormous pores dotting his nose and cheeks.

Just as I asked the question, he made a face like he'd crunched on a bit of bone.

"What's the matter? Are you okay?" I watched with concern. His facial expression wasn't improving.

He shook his head, nose wrinkling. "Potato salad tastes off."

I watched him wipe his fork clean with his napkin and then glance at my own plate where a plop of the salad sat on a lettuce leaf.

"Don't eat that," he advised, shaking his head.

"Really?" I asked, dipping a tine of my fork into the mayonnaise mixture. I brought it to my nose and gave a quick sniff, but it smelled normal to me.

He took a gulp of water. "Definitely off. In fact, we should tell the caterers to clear it away before anyone else eats it."

There was a cough from the front of the table. Ian waved his napkin in front of his face. He smiled weakly at whatever Gordon, the neighbor, was saying, and gestured with his hand that he'd be right back. He took a big drink of wine, grimaced again, and stood with a scrape of the chair legs against the wood floor. Ian's face glistened with sweat. He had that green around the gills look, and I thought he might vomit, to be honest.

Celeste tapped my elbow. "He doesn't look like he feels very well." She poked at her barbecue chicken. "I hope it's not something in the food."

I glanced at the potato salad. Besides my neighbor, everyone else had eaten it and seemed to be okay. "Maybe it's a virus," I said.

She nodded. "The stomach flu does seem to be going around." Still, she laid the heavy silver fork on the plate with a soft clink. "Now, about your mother."

I stared at Uncle Chris, hoping for a lifeline.

He must have felt my eyes on him. "How you doing down there, ladies?" he asked.

Celeste answered, "I was just telling Stella that I think Ruth, Ian's mom, is here wishing him well tonight. Don't you think so, Jasmine? That she's here, lurking around the corners, keeping an eye on things?"

Everyone around the table quieted at the strange statement. I wondered what kind of crazy thing she was going to say next.

Jasmine's eyes widened in surprise. "Well, I... I don't quite know about that."

"Oh, they come and check in, especially on momentous occasions. Life. Going away parties. Death." Celeste tittered. "You know that cold feeling rising along the back of your neck when you are convinced someone is watching you? And you spin around, hoping to catch them, but no one is there?" She winked. "That's the spirits checking on you from the other side."

Now, I considered if Celeste might be drunk.

Jasmine didn't seem to know how to answer that. "That very well could be." She twisted a napkin and tossed it on her plate. "If you will excuse me." She got up and moved stiffly through the doorway in the direction that Ian went.

I turned back to my potato salad. This party exemplified everything I hated about crowds, stuck as I was between two doozy conversationalists. Concentrating on my plate felt like the safest option by far.

My peace didn't last for long.

"You know," said Celeste, brushing my elbow again. "I'm sensing a spiritual presence for sure."

"I told you the salad was no good," grumbled the man on my right. "Poor guy is probably puking his guts out."

"They can make themselves visible if they want," continued Celeste.

"Just hope it doesn't happen to me," growled the man.

At that moment, Jasmine re-entered the room with a smile.

"Is he okay?" asked the neighbor's wife.

"He's just freshening up," she said to the entire table.

"Well, that's good news," said Celeste, while my neighbor frowned discontentedly, apparently preferring the visual of Ian being sick.

The servers cleared the plates and then dessert was offered, chocolate mousse and French silk pie. I was stuffed and passed. Besides, I couldn't tell if it was the idea put into my head by both my neighbor and Celeste, but I was feeling a little queasy.

"Poor Jasmine, being forced to move," Celeste said again. I was scared to give her my attention, unsure of what topic she would start in on next.

"I heard it was a great move for them," I finally answered.

"She loves this house. She'd never dreamed of leaving it. No, he's forcing her." She went back to spooning up her dessert. She tasted the dot of chocolate at the end of the spoon before putting down the utensil. I realized I'd scarcely seen her eat a thing.

I hardly knew how to answer that, and decided to nod and focus on my wine. Across from me, Kari seemed to be feeling great. She laughed at whatever the neighbor's wife said to her and finished her wine.

But when the servers came later to removed the dessert

plates, I think we all eyed Ian's empty seat. It was a weird feeling, not knowing exactly what to do with the guest of honor absent. Do we get up and mingle? Sit and wait?

Jasmine glanced nervously back in the hall's direction, clearly surprised Ian wasn't back. Finally, Uncle Chris balled up his napkin and stood up. "I'll just go check on him."

Jasmine seemed reassured and dipped her head in a graceful nod. An uneasy feeling curled inside of me, the kind that brought to mind old TV shows that my dad used to love where they threw salt over their shoulder while muttering about dark signs. So it was with sinking dread, but no surprise, when Uncle Chris returned, gray-faced. "Call the police," he demanded.

"The police?" gasped the neighbor, Gordon.

"Is it Ian? Is he not well? Should I call an ambulance?" Jasmine jumped up and gripped the table. The blood drained from her face, allowing her lips to stand out like raspberries on ice-cream.

Uncle Chris faced her. He exhaled deeply and the lines around his mouth deepened. "I'm sorry, Jasmine. An ambulance won't help him now. He's dead."

Gasps and screams of shock rose around the table. I stared in disbelief toward Jasmine.

Her eyes rolled back in her head, and she fainted, nearly hitting her head on the table. Somehow Uncle Chris managed to catch her before that happened and eased her to the floor.

THE POLICE ARRIVED a short time later. They quarantined us into separate groups where we were all questioned. It surprised me when Officer Carlson arrived. We'd run into each other a few times now, over the course of the time since I'd moved to Brookfield. I don't think I was one of his favorite people. In fact, he'd made fun of me and called me Hollywood because I was from the west coast. I'd sarcastically mentioned that Washington was not California, but he didn't seem to care.

His eyes widened when he saw me, and then he turned to mutter at his partner. Of course, it was loud enough for me to hear. "I'm too close to her to interview her." The two of them laughed.

I didn't like what his buddy thought Carlson inferred, and Carlson didn't seem to correct it. I crossed my arms, my face settling into the same scowl I'd used when staring down mocking competitors at a track meet in high school.

Officer Carlson walked away, and his partner beckoned me

over to him. I stalked over with more attitude than one should have when the guest of honor has died at a party.

"I'm Officer Daniels, and I have just a few questions. So, please set the scene for me, where were you during the dinner?" he asked, staring me straight in the eye. Officer Carlson was tall and bald, but his partner was a short guy. Officer Daniels didn't have much more hair than Carlson though. However, Officer Carlson's bald head was by choice rather than nature—and Daniels seemed to desperately be hanging on to his fringe from the looks of the hair wax.

"I was at the table," I succinctly answered. I'd learned in my past dealings with the police to limit the details I offered.

He took out a pad and used his teeth to pull off the cap. "Did you see Ian leave?"

"Yes. He seemed sick."

"So he left the table to...?" He raised an eyebrow, waiting for me to fill in the blank.

I shrugged. "I'm not sure why he left. Maybe to go to the bathroom?"

From the corner of my eye, I saw Uncle Chris talking with another officer. His pale face showed how he was still in shock, and I felt sorry for him.

"What did you think when Ian didn't return to the table?" the officer asked.

"I thought nothing of it, because his wife got up and checked on him. She said he was fine, just freshening up."

"So, what made you think he might have gotten sick?"

I started to mention the potato salad, but that would put the focus on Kari. I shrugged instead. "Everyone has weird food allergies nowadays. You never know what will affect a person."

"Did anyone else notice he was gone?"

"I think we all did. I heard that lady over there ask Ian's wife if he was okay. Maybe that's what made me wonder if he had become sick."

"And what did his wife say?"

"Jasmine said she was sure he'd be right back."

"Did Jasmine act suspiciously in any way?"

That jerked me upright. "What do you mean?"

"I mean, was her behavior in any way suspicious? Did it seem like she was trying to delay people looking for him, etcetera?"

My eyebrows raised, shocked he was asking me, but I shook my head. "No. I think she checked on him after being concerned, but she herself was reassured after she'd talked with him." I narrowed my eyes. "Why are you asking these questions? What exactly happened to him?"

Officer Daniels ignored me. "Was there anyone else that caught your attention by acting strangely?"

Again, I shook my head, breathing deep to remain calm. It occurred to me that every person here was being asked the same questions. What if someone thought *I'd* done something suspicious?

He snapped the notebook shut. "We might like you to come down to the station at some point, so stick around town."

"Why would you need me to come down?" I asked.

"To get your fingerprints. We don't know the cause of death yet."

I clenched my hands when he said this. He noticed and lifted an eyebrow as he flipped open the pad to scribble some more. Great. Now, what did he write? And why was I suddenly feeling guilty? Heat crawled up under my collar and filled my face. I could just imagine that my cheeks were glowing like stop signs.

"Thank you for your cooperation, Miss O'Neil. That will be all for now." He glanced around the place. "Is anyone staying behind to clean up? It looks like Mrs. Stuber will need some help."

Punctuating that statement was a sob that Jasmine let out as the neighbor's wife hugged her. "Yes, I will." I rubbed the back of my neck, still amazed to be caught up in all of this.

Officer Daniels walked over to Celeste while I headed toward Uncle Chris. A balloon bobbed in my way, and I batted it down. Uncle Chris was talking with one of the guys that both he and Ian had graduated with.

"How you holding up?" he asked and pulled me in with a heavy arm over my shoulders.

I patted his back. "I was coming over here to ask you the same thing. How are you?"

His lips pressed together, and I saw he couldn't speak. He shook his head and then stared out the window, his eyes bloodshot.

"I'm so sorry," I said, hugging him tighter.

"Yeah, Ian was a good guy," said the other man standing there. "By the way, I'm Mike."

I nodded in his direction while Uncle Chris croaked out, "Ian was one of the best. I don't know how Jasmine will manage without him."

"How long have they been married?" I asked.

"Oh, just over a year."

"But they've dated for a while," Mike interjected.

"Yeah, they've been on and off for a few years," Uncle Chris amended.

"I see. Do they have kids?" I asked.

"No."

"He never wanted any."

"Well, people change," I said.

"Not him. He's said that for as long as I've known him." Uncle Chris pulled out a cigar. He stared at it longingly and rolled it in his hands.

"No kids that we *know* of," Mike said, with a soft chuckle. "You know how Ian was. I'm sure there's a few out there."

"He was a playboy, huh?" That shouldn't surprise me. Uncle Chris was an overgrown frat boy, himself.

"Let's just say he was well-known for his dalliances," Mike answered.

"Quite the horn dog," interjected Uncle Chris.

"But he settled down once he met Jasmine, huh?" I clarified, feeling slightly concerned. Can leopards change their spots?

"Well, I think that was part of the problem, why they broke

up so many times. But I'm sure he's been on the straight and narrow ever since they've been married." Mike nodded.

"How she managed to lock him down, I'll never know," Uncle Chris said. "Of course, marriage is not for me."

"How about love?" I asked.

"They definitely did love each other. Traveled the world together so far."

"Really!"

"Yeah. I can't believe he's gone." Uncle Chris sighed. He glanced around at the house. "Everything's a mess."

"What do you mean?"

"I mean the will is going to have to be sorted out, there are new buyers who signed a contract that we'll have to deal with. I don't know where Jasmine is going to go."

"Can any of the contracts be voided in light of what happened?"

"We'll see," Uncle Chris said. "I know she never wanted to move in the first place."

People began leaving as the police were done interviewing them. It hit me hard that I would soon be alone with the grieving new widow.

3

*A*nd, just like that, everyone had filtered out. Not in
a rush, so you would notice an empty room. More
like a trickle, like a slow helium balloon leak, that became
obvious once the balloon settled to the floor. All of the family
friends, the police, and emergency personnel. Even the
caterers abandoned us, taking their silver tureens away. In
fact, I think they were the first to go.

Uncle Chris sat with Jasmine in the other room, accompanied
by Celeste. I could hear Jasmine on the phone. Her tears were
chilling.

Kari and I stared at each other over the table still littered with
wine glasses and China. Without another word, we both
began to clean up. It was incredibly somber and surreal to

clear the remnants of a celebration that had so abruptly turned into tragedy.

"What are you thinking?" Kari whispered.

I understood why she whispered. Even though Jasmine was down the hall in the other room, it felt almost sacrilegious to speak out-loud. "I'm thinking we're all in shock." I gathered up the cloth napkins.

"Do you think it was a heart attack?" she asked. "Apoplexy?"

"Apoplexy? That's a real thing? I thought that was just something the doctor shouted in the 16th century before he brought out the leeches."

"It's a real thing," she whispered. Another wail rose from the living room, making me shiver.

"I have no idea," I answered, grabbing the silverware. She stacked the plates, and we headed into the kitchen.

The kitchen provided enough of a buffer that we could no longer hear Jasmine's grief. A sweet scent filled the air, not of barbecue, but of something else. Something I couldn't identify.

"It's the diffuser," Kari said, noting how I was sniffing the air. She pointed to an unassuming little vase that was spraying a fine mist in the air. "I have that oil. Cozy Home."

The counter was littered with aluminum trays of meat, potatoes, salads, and vegetables. It seemed the caterers decided to cut their losses and split as soon as the cops showed up. I couldn't blame them.

I groaned. "What a mess. Who needs twenty pounds of ribs? Or this lasagna pan of bacon and green beans? There's enough food left to feed an army."

"I can't believe the caterer's abandoned us. They sure tore out of Dodge when the cops arrived." She shook her head at the mess. "I say we wrap it and pile it in the fridge. I'm guessing there's going to be a lot of people coming over."

We jumped into gear, her wrapping the food and me washing dishes.

She leaned over and whispered again, "You don't suppose it was murder?"

"Murder?" Her question should have been more shocking, but Ian's death still felt packed in a surreal bubble. Besides, we *had* been interviewed by the police.

Still, I was scared to answer. What if Jasmine overheard?

Kari ripped off a piece of plastic wrap. Immediately it balled. Huffing, she tossed it to one side and tried again. "Like maybe his neighbor," she whispered. "He kept giving Ian funny looks throughout dinner."

"Gordon?" I asked. "Ian seemed kind of surprised when he showed up."

"That was weird. Gordon and Ian didn't get along. Something about Christmas lights or dogs in each other's yards. Your uncle was a little worried when he hung up the flamingo sign, sure that Gordon Taylor and his wife would start complaining. But maybe, they were relieved that Ian and Jasmine were moving away."

"Yeah. They have little motive. What about the new buyers?" I asked, dumping wine from a glass down the drain. My nose wrinkled at the especially sour scent.

"They have the least motive of all," Kari stated adamantly. "No, we need to figure out who would have benefited the most."

No one obvious came to mind. Then again, I hardly knew the man. The vaporizer spritzed as I wiped the surrounding counter. It really smelled good. I found the oil behind the diffuser, along with a bottle of antacid on the counter.

"You think Jasmine needs this? I don't want this to get lost in the shuffle."

"Maybe move it over here." She opened a few of the cupboards. "Shoot. No luck. I usually keep medicine above my fridge."

"I'll leave it here. Someone can put it away later." I set the container next to the sink and went back to wiping the crumbs into my hand. Kari probably thought I was being quiet, but my brain was in overdrive, trying to analyze all the conversations that had happened at the table. Nothing seemed out of place. In fact, aside from my sick neighbor, most everyone had seemed happy. No surprise there. Wasn't it usually that way at a party?

Kari rinsed off the serving spoons. "You know that tall bald cop? He told me to stick around town." She stuck them in the dishwasher and then dried her hands.

My eyes widened. "His partner told me the same thing!"

Her cheeks puffed and she shook her head. "Weird and weirder." She ripped off another piece of plastic wrap and grabbed the potato salad.

I eyed it nervously. "Do you think it's still good?"

"Good? It's the bomb, girlfriend. Everyone says their homemade potato salad is the best." She smiled smugly. "But mine really is. Besides, why wouldn't it be?"

"I mean because it's been out at room temperature for so long." It wasn't just my neighbor that had a problem. I'd seen Ian take a bite of something and then grimace and quickly drink his wine."

"For the amount of work this took, I'm going to chance it. Joe will eat it. He's got an iron gut." She wrapped it firmly.

I wrinkled my nose. I wasn't a big potato salad partaker at the best of times, but especially not after someone had died.

She continued to load the dishwasher while I gathered the linen napkins from the end of the counter where I'd left them. My hope was that there was a laundry room nearby.

I headed down the hall, away from the living room and towards several promising doors. I could hear Uncle Chris again. And was that the neighbor, Gordon?

The first door turned out to be the entrance to a study. It was stuffed with books and leather furniture and a huge desk. I quickly shut it and opened the next.

This one was the bathroom. It was a huge room, decorated in the colors of rust and cream, and brass fixtures. Someone had thrown a hand towel on the quartz counter that was splashed with water. Another lay on the floor. I decided to tidy it a bit, first hanging the towels and then using some toilet paper to wipe down the counter.

I was about to throw the wad of toilet paper in the wicker trash can when I saw a little gold clasp on the floor. I picked it up, meaning to leave it on the counter.

A cold breeze brushed against my cheek. There was a squeak in the floorboard behind me.

Every hair on my neck rose.

Someone was watching me. It was happening just like Celeste described. Goosebumps trickled down my spine. The air suddenly felt heavy, like the humidity in a steam room. Slowly, I straightened and glanced in the mirror, dreading to see what was behind me.

Light from the hallway reflected in the glass, and then I saw a door. It was open and directly across the hall from me. The interior was dark, and I couldn't see who was in there. Watching me. My hand trembled with the urge to slam the bathroom door closed. To lock myself safely away. Instead, heart pounding, I spun around and boldly walked across the hallway.

"Hello?" I called at the room's entrance. My voice scared me to hear it cut through the silence, as weird as that sounds.

There was no answer. I nudged the door open a bit more. A hum made me nearly jump out of my skin until I realized it was a wine fridge.

It was the butler's pantry. I walked inside to see a long counter, cupboards, even a small sink. There was another door on the other end that was slowly closing. I strode over and shoved it open.

I entered the kitchen. There was no one in there.

What in the world? Where did they go?

Quickly, I ran past the granite counters and entered the dining room.

"What are we supposed to do with these?" Kari asked, standing by the table with a bouquet of helium balloons.

"Did you see someone come through here?" I asked, feeling breathless.

She watched me like I had a koala bear hanging off my head. I stopped dead in my tracks feeling foolish at my over-reaction.

"What do you mean?" she asked, pausing from winding the ribbons around her hand. "You okay?"

"Someone was watching me while I was straightening the bathroom. I'm trying to figure out who it was."

"The bathroom?" She bit her lip, eyes wide. "Did you know that's where they found Ian?"

"What?" I shivered. It hadn't occurred to me. Had the towel been on the floor because he'd felt faint, perhaps grabbing for the counter for balance?

Nausea roiled through me.

"Today, when your Uncle found him. Ian was in the

bathroom. Oh, my gosh. Do you think Ian was like…hanging around still? Maybe he hasn't left yet."

I stared at her. "Are you telling me it was a ghost?"

"Well, there's no one here but us, besides the three in the living room. Unless, I mean, maybe you imagined it. You know, here's this creepy house where someone just died… I've been kind of spooked myself."

I liked that explanation better and nodded. "Yeah. Of course, that's it. I'm tired, and it's been a long day. My nerves are probably on overload."

She nodded. "We both need to get home. Now, tell me what I'm supposed to do with these? We can't leave them here." She tugged on the balloons, making them bob against each other.

"Maybe your kids want them?" I suggested.

She blinked incredulous eyes at me. "Death balloons, Stella. You're offering my kids death balloons."

"Oh! Oops!" I thought for a second. "Maybe the hospital would like them? Or the nursing home?"

She nodded. "Great idea. I'll put them in your car."

I had to smile at how slick she was.

As she headed outside, I realized I was still clutching that darn pile of napkins. I wasn't too keen to take a second trip down the hallway. Still, I wasn't going to let my imagination dictate to me. However, as I passed it, I did shut the door to the butler's pantry.

The laundry room was next to it, with sleek silver-gray machines, complete with a steaming rack and an ironing center. I admired the dryer, my own rental house only had a wooden rack to dry clothes, and examined the bead-board on the walls. It was darn cute. I was working on the rental in exchange for rent, and I thought that would be an incredible addition to my own little laundry room. I chucked the napkins into one of the baskets I found and then headed back to the kitchen.

Kari was wiping out the sink. I found a broom and swept while she finished, and then we were done.

"Now what?" I asked.

"Let's get out of here," Kari answered.

Sounded good to me. I searched for my jacket with my thoughts scattered like a box of puzzle pieces, everything from death, potato salad, and oddly enough, paint colors.

Kari swept the bowl and purse into her arms and we headed out. As we entered the hallway, my attention focused—in a guilty eaves-droppery way— onto the living room. I was afraid of what I might hear, to be honest, and my stomach clenched.

Instead of the expected crying, there was a peal of laughter. What in the world? I knew that Uncle Chris was good at lightening up the mood, but maybe he was taking his job too seriously here.

The laughter started again, and Kari and I stared at each other with raised eyebrows.

"Oh, Gordon. What would I do without you?" Jasmine giggled.

I paused, caught in the words. What did that mean?

Kari grabbed my arm and pulled me through the front door.

"Sorry," she said. "I saw someone's shadow and didn't want either of us to get caught snooping."

"Thanks for the save," I said gratefully, following her down the driveway. She juggled her salad into her other arm and dug through her purse for her keys. I was on the simple plan, a thin wallet in my back pocket, and keys in my jacket.

Huffing a bit, she opened the trunk before hurling the potato salad inside. I blinked in surprise at the abuse that salad was going through. Knowing it would be eaten at the end of the journey made me want to hurl. I gave her a shivery goodbye and hopped into my car.

Balloons bopped me in my face. I'd forgotten Kari had said she'd put them in my car and she sure did. I pushed them out of the passenger seat and into the rear where they bobbled until they managed to cover up every last bit of rear window.

Amazing. I fastened my seat belt as Kari drove by. She gave a little toot of her van horn and a waggle of her fingers. I swear her grin was evil.

I rolled my eyes and carefully backed out using my side mirrors and then headed to the nursing home.

I could have never expected who I was going to see there.

4

I walked into the nursing home with the bouquet of balloons. I'd narrowly avoided having a Mary Poppins moment when a gust of wind grabbed them, nearly lifting me off my feet. Luckily, I managed to wrangle them back to earth with them bopping me in the face and winding their ribbons around my body. It was with pure relief that I dropped them off at the front desk. The nurse seemed happy to receive them. At least that's how I was choosing to interpret the dour frown she gave me when I left her holding the bouquet. I hurried to leave when a surprised yell stopped me.

"Stella! Yoohoo!"

I turned slowly, terrified that the nurse had somehow

discovered my name. She was going to make me take those balloons back, wasn't she?

Imagine my surprise when I discovered that it was Charity Valentine, a senior woman who had once been my client. To say things hadn't gone well would be the understatement of the century, and my heart leaped into my throat when I saw her here. I knew that both she and her older sister had been looking for a new house. Was she now a resident of the nursing home?

And was this my fault?

She scampered over—all four feet of her— as spry as I remembered. Her curls bobbed around her face. "How very good to see you," she squealed, grabbing my hand.

It was then that I noticed a purple badge on her shoulder, stating "volunteer." The relief that flooded through me made me giddy. "Charity! Don't you look wonderful! Do you work here?"

"I do, I do. I came here a few weeks ago to drop off flowers and then met a dear old classmate of mine. Stella! I have a beau!" " She blushed and giggled behind her hand.

Her joy was contagious. "I'm so happy for you!"

"Yes! And you'll never guess. He and I are now in charge of the dance lessons! Right now we are teaching the fox-trot."

We chatted some more, with me carefully skirting the subject of her older sister. The elder Ms. Valentine's last name almost seemed like an oxymoron because of her baleful attitude. After a few minutes, I left Charity to go find her man. Seriously, it brought some suspicious stinging to my eyes to watch her hurry away. She'd waited such a long time to have a special someone, and I was delighted for her.

I returned to my car in a rather introspective mood. The circle of life was flashing its display all around me. Love. Death. Family. The problem was, I couldn't decide exactly where I was in the circle. Was I just... existing?

I groaned at the heavy thought. Trust me to get all melancholy and deep about a friend finally finding love. I could tell it was no good to go straight home. I'd just spiral. There was only one place I knew I could go when I was in this type of mood; my grandfather Oscar's place.

Deciding to visit him, I shifted the car into drive. As I pulled onto the highway, the phone rang. Another groan escaped me as I read the name.

Dad. I bet he already knew what had just happened at the party. Don't ask me how. He always had a sixth sense about stuff like this. Either that or he had a hoard of spies. Knowing the stock he came from, that was always a possibility.

I couldn't think about spies now, resigning myself to answer.

It's funny how sometimes when you need to talk, the exact wrong person appears. It's not that I didn't love my dad. I adored him. It's just that he's not always helpful.

"Hi, Dad."

His voice boomed through the car's speakers. "Stella, I just heard what happened. Are you okay?" His voice was tight with concern.

"Yeah. I'm kind of in shock right now." I clenched the steering wheel and had to remind myself to ease up and relax.

"What I want to know is how this happened? What kinds of places is my brother dragging you to? Parties with dead bodies? I knew you moving out there was a bad idea."

"Dad, I don't know what you're thinking, but it wasn't like that. They were friends. Uncle Chris was throwing him a going away party."

"Oh, I know all about your uncle's friends. Were they drinking? Drugs?"

I bit my lip. This was exactly what I'd feared would happen. Dad was treating me like a kid again. "It was a respectable party. I mean, other than the shock of a man dying. This was Uncle Chris's friend, Dad. I think you could be more understanding."

He sighed, his breath echoing through the speakers, and

blanketing me with his disapproval. "Stella, can you just explain something to me?"

Tightness squeezed my chest. Here it comes. The lecture. "I'll try. What is it?"

The two seconds interim seemed to last forever as I tried to prepare myself for the onslaught of his questions.

"I just don't understand why you're doing it," he finally said.

"Doing what?"

"Living out there on a small salary when you had everything you could have wanted out here. Heck, I can even get your job back if you'd just return. You had money, you had respect. You had a good career. What happened to you? It's like I don't even know you anymore."

Oh, boy. That hurt. This wasn't the first time he'd question why I'd moved back to Pennsylvania. And, thus far, he'd never accepted my answer.

"Was it just Oscar? You wanted to meet him?" Bitterness threaded through his voice. He'd never divulged the reason he'd cut his dad off, but I could tell that my dad thought I'd betrayed him by moving back.

"No, Dad. That's not it. I mean, that was part of it, but I could have just flown down for a visit if that's what I wanted. I do have a lot of curiosity and questions about my family

45

though. It's just been you and me for so long. Growing up, everyone I knew had a family. I was the weirdo without one. And there is one out here. So, I needed to figure that out."

"So it was for him." He sighed.

"Not just him." I sucked in a deep breath and then blurted out. "I'm so honored to be compared to you in so many ways. When people say I'm honest or have high integrity like you that makes me happier than you will ever know. But I'm not like you in the need for a career. I'm actually really thankful for this realty job. It's been interesting."

A big semi roared past me, scaring me. I jerked in my seat and told myself to calm down. The seconds ticked by as I waited to hear how he would respond.

His voice was glum. "I thought I'd be doing better with you living out there. I just can't seem to accept your decision."

I swallowed, not knowing how to make him feel better.

"All right kiddo, I'll talk with you later. Stay safe."

"I will, Dad."

"Love you."

"I love you, too."

We hung up with me feeling hollow and somehow guilty. I was in no better mood when I pulled down Oscar's driveway.

Across the hedge that divided his property from the neighbors, I spotted a gal about my age jump down the steps of a huge house and get into a white van. The van gave a loud pop, and then she backed up as I shut my car door. For a second, our eyes met, and she gave a cheery wave.

I knew that house was the Baker Street Bed-and-Breakfast. I'd seen the van there before and wondered who she was. She seemed nice. Friendly.

I felt more alone in the world than I'd felt in a long time.

A gust of wind blew my hair in my eyes. I tucked it back and hurried over to the old porch.

So much drama. I wish I knew exactly why both my uncle and my dad wouldn't talk with Oscar. I'd been working hard to bring the family back together, and I'd thought I'd made progress. Today's conversation with Dad kind of put a damper on my dreams of a big family reunion in the near future.

I knocked on the door and then rubbed my hands together from the cold. As expected, a puffy tornado raced down the hallway, yapping a mile a minute. Peanut, or Bear as Oscar liked to call her, was my late grandmother's Pomeranian. She jumped on the glass window next to the door and panted, before looking back toward the living room and giving an excited bark. I think in dog language, she was yelling, "Hurry, old man! The treat-giver's at the door!"

The old man was listening because he appeared around the corner. Slowly, he shuffled down the hallway. I could practically hear his worn flannel slippers scuffing against the hardwood. His face was set in a scowl—the man did not like to show any other emotion—but he couldn't fool me. I saw a twinkle in his eye and a giddy-up in his step that he normally didn't have.

He opened the door and stared up at me through thick glasses. "What do you want?" he said gruffly.

I had no time to answer. Peanut shot out like a rocket and was now dancing around my feet.

"Come here, come here, come here," I said, bouncing around, trying to catch the fluff-nugget. Finally, I scooped her up and stood to meet Oscar rolling his eyes.

"That dagnabbit dog. Always has to be front and center like she's the princess at the ball."

"Well, she is a princess, aren't you girl." I kissed her head, and Peanut returned the favor by licking my cheek.

"You here for a 'talking moment?' I was expecting you. Coffee's on."

It blew my mind to hear him use his reference word that

meant needing a sounding board. "How'd you know I was on my way?" It was a curious thing. He always seemed to read my mind.

"Police scanner," Oscar pointed to an antiquated black box. He didn't say more, just shuffled into the kitchen. I followed after him, cuddling the dog. Her weight in my arms and soft fur against my cheek was the comfort I needed. I buried my face in and sighed, thankful for dogs.

Just inside the entrance of the old craftsman home, was a hallway lined with pictures. Each one placed perfectly next to the other on an invisible parallel line that suggested orderliness, yet the frames were covered in dust to the point of appearing furry.

I stopped before the first photo. It was of Oscar and my grandmother. They stood in front of a palm tree with young grins in some tropical location that suggested the first blush of marriage.

Following that was one of them holding a baby—my father. I remember the first time I'd seen it. When Dad packed up to move us to Washington, he truly left his old life behind, and I'd never seen him as an infant or child. It had been kind of shocking, as ridiculous as it sounds, to see evidence that he'd once been young like me.

The next picture was of my father in a little sailor suit, and a new baby, Uncle Chris. Uncle Chris had been a fat baby and was nearly bursting out of his own sailor suit. Grandma smiled contentedly as she held the roly-poly boy.

But my dad stared with eyes dark and serious. It made me want to scoop him up and play catch with him, or give him an ice-cream cone. Something to make him smile.

The next few pictures recorded Uncle Chris and my dad's journey through school. The row ended with two college graduation photos. Uncle Chris was true to form as he made a goofy face at the camera.

In Dad's graduation picture, I detected a difference from the solemn pictures of his youth and the serious man he was today. In this one, he had an easy-going smile on his face, and his eyes appeared lighter. I recalled that this was around the time he'd met my mother. Was it because he'd finally had his degree and could move on with his life that had brought him such joy?

Or was it my mom?

I touched the frame as bittersweetness fluttered in my heart like a strange butterfly. Love. I can't say I'd really experienced it, at least not much more than the tiny flickers that had promised something deeper, but had soon sputtered out. Seeing my dad's face in this photo made me think there really was something about true love...and maybe he'd found it with my mom.

"You coming in or trying to grow roots?" Oscar hollered.

"Coming!" I called. I kissed Peanut's head one more time. "Her fur is shorter," I commented as I walked into the kitchen.

"She went to the dog groomers. Georgie took her."

"Georgie?" I asked, setting the dog down and taking off my coat. I hung it on the back of one of the farm chairs.

"Georgie." He jerked his thumb in the direction of the house next door. "My new Hot Thing's granddaughter."

Ewww. I shivered. That was one expression I never needed to hear again. Rapidly, I changed the subject.

"So, you know why I'm here? From the scanner?"

"Yeah, I was expecting you." He shambled over with a cup of coffee and a plate of toast. "Go on, sit on your biscuit and let it out."

I smiled and sat down. He always had a way of disarming me by lightening the mood but still creating a safe space to talk. "So did you know it was Uncle Chris's friend? Ian Stuber."

He grunted in surprise.

As I talked, he trekked back and forth to the table with butter, sugar, a pot of jelly, and finally his own mug of coffee. There was no offer of cream. I highly doubted he had any milk that wasn't a solid chunk in his fridge, anyway.

Oscar sat down with a huff and Peanut immediately sprang to his feet. "Do they suspect foul play?"

"The cops did ask a few questions. We were all together at the table, so I don't see how it would be a possibility. I think it had to have been a reaction to something he ate."

"Best way murder happens." He pointed a half-eaten toast triangle at me. "You have an alibi. Guy dies out of sight."

I shivered and rubbed my arms. "I didn't see anything unusual. We were all eating the same thing. Even Kari's potato salad."

He glanced up then. "Something wrong with the salad?"

"I didn't eat any, but the guy next to me said it was off. And Ian did sort of grimace before he got up and left the table."

"Who was at this party?" Oscar's eyebrows beetled down.

I named off those who I remembered.

"Gordon Taylor?" he said with a grunt. "That guy's a load of trouble."

5

"Trouble? How do you know about Gordon Taylor?" Yeah, I went straight to the point, but Oscar appreciated it when you didn't pull any punches.

"It was a dark and spooky night," he began.

My eyebrow flickered, but he was being serious. He patted his lap for Peanut to jump up. "I was on a stakeout—one of my last ones. Before my darling wife got sick." He winced as he mentioned his late wife. "We were trying to take a dirty informant into protective custody. Hector was a mob enforcer, and he got there before us. And, let's just say, Hector was thorough and left little behind for us to find. Gordon Taylor was Hector's friend."

"Oh, wow." I sat, a little stunned. The poky couple who

showed up late at the party sure didn't look like people with mob ties. "Do you think the police who showed up at Ian's house know?"

"Anyone worth their salt in law enforcement knows. They have an eye on him, you can bet on that. If foul play happened, Gordon's the one I'd suspect."

Well, that was a thunderclap of news.

"Gordon and his wife did seem to arrive unexpectedly. I'd heard Gordon and Ian didn't always get along, which made our dealings with selling the house tricky. We thought they'd throw a fit about the Flamingo Realty sign. Still, everything seemed to go all right after they came. They even brought wine."

"Wine?" His voice was full of suspicion.

I shook my head. "It was a sealed bottle."

He shrugged and sipped his coffee. "You know where my vote's going. The police must suspect something to interview all of you like that."

I spun my mug on the table as a little worm of worry grew in my head. Oscar pulled out a newspaper—one of the few people I knew who still read them. Finally, I pulled out my phone and started fielding emails.

We sat in comfortable silence, broken only by the ticking of what he'd once informed me was a malfunctioning cuckoo clock (but it's right twice a day, he said adamantly) and the rattling of the refrigerator. As an introvert, the silence suited me. Quite a bit of time slipped by, with me lulled into relaxation by the peace. I stretched and glanced over to see him working at the crossword puzzle.

"I guess I should go," I said with a sigh.

"Storm's coming. You drive safe, you hear?" He eyed me over the top of his glasses.

I nodded and gave him a half-hug, which Peanut interrupted by abruptly jumping up from his lap and jabbing her nose into my face.

His warning was no joke. As soon as I left his house, I could see black clouds crowding together in the sky. The snow started before I even made it home, falling, not in those soft floating flakes that looked like feathers off an angel's wing, but the kind that made little ticks on the window. I was thankful to pull into my driveway. I hurried in the house and immediately searched for a sweater. The old house was drafty. I ended up dressing in pajamas with a blanket snuggled around my shoulders for good measure.

Okay, it was time to chill out before bed. I thought I might check out my Great-great Grandma Wiktoria's letters.

The antique letters were a gift from my dad, who'd sent them in a care package a few months back. Grandma Wiktoria had escaped Poland when Hitler was overtaking the country. These were the letters she'd written to her mother who she had to leave behind.

Unfortunately, they were all written in Polish, so it had been slow going to interpret them. I pulled out the last one I'd managed to translate, using an app, and curled up on my bed with a pen and a pad of paper.

Taking the cap off the pen, I gently smoothed out the letter, while chewing on the cap. It was not nearly as satisfying to bite as a pencil, where the soft wood would give under my teeth in neat little dents, but it helped me focus. Back in grade school, I was always in trouble for ruining my pencils, but that's another story.

Her letter began like this...

DEAREST MOTHER,

It's spring here. I remember the springtime back in Krakow. How fresh the beautiful mountain air is of the High Tatras. I miss you so much, yet at times, I can almost feel you with me. It's your prayers, maybe? Or your thoughts. Either way, I swear I can nearly feel your hug. There isn't a day that has gone by that I don't hear your admonishments or encouragement. I miss you so.

. . .

I SET the letter down on the worn quilt. Wiktoria's words rang through my head. I could hear the pain of missing her mother. She'd been so strong to start this new life in America despite everything she left behind. Closing my eyes, I leaned my head back against the pillow. Everyone seemed to have it all figured out, while here I was, still trying to discover the depths of what made me—me. Today, for example, I was at the party, feeling confident and secure. Finally, feeling like I had it all together, like I'd achieved being a grown-up. When, suddenly, a comment from a stranger ripped apart what was apparently a facade and exposed me as this insecure little girl who missed her mom.

Celeste had knocked me for a loop, that's for sure. I blushed as I remembered struggling to rise above the tidal wave of emotions to give her my usual excuse about my lack of a mom. My stammering words were flimsy like this piece of paper in my hand. My emotions tattered.

At this moment, I felt like I couldn't face ever being asked that question again.

And yet it was being asked. By me this time. In a little girl voice, and then an adult woman voice, insecure, and confused. *Why did you go, Mom?*

Was it possible she had... died?

Celeste made that weird comment about Ian's mom coming back to visit him. All boogey-woogey—just too weird.

Still, if my mom had died, was she watching me? I mean, there wasn't a chance that it was her that I'd felt when I was in Ian's bathroom, was there?

I shook my head, feeling silly. *I need to go to bed, stat. This day has me so wound up, I'm not even making sense anymore.*

Still, my questions showed that it was high time to have a real conversation about all of this with Dad. It was ridiculous that I, as a grown woman, had never talked to him about her.

Dad seemed so in control, such a type A personality who always had it together. But there was a vulnerability in him concerning my mom that nearly broke him. I'd seen it in his face through wrinkles of grief and wet tracks of tears when I was little, and I'd vowed then I'd take care of him so he'd never feel that way again.

Of course, when I'd made the vow, I was only a little girl. Maybe five or six. I hadn't known then that my father didn't need the security a little girl could bring. Still, I'd always felt my role was to make him proud. To show him that I was enough to make us happy.

To make him never miss my mom again.

I sighed now, a big heaving one. My throat felt tight and my eyes burned.

I'd never realized before this moment just what a heavy burden that had been.

I twirled the letter in my hand. Why did Dad cut Grandpa off? I mean, I know the reasons he gave me, the man was evil, a family destroyer, always moving them from place to place. Dad had also been resentful because grandma used to beg Oscar to quit the FBI and Oscar wouldn't.

All those reasons had been enough for me to accept the division for years. But now, thinking about it, seriously thinking about it, I felt like I was missing a huge piece of the mystery.

And not only had Dad cut off Oscar, he had never been all that close to Uncle Chris either.

Oscar. I smiled as I thought of him. I didn't call him grandpa —he hadn't invited me to, and I sure didn't feel comfortable. But he was a new gift in my life. My own flesh and blood, a history that extended past just my father and me.

I rolled over, springs squeaking underneath me in the ancient mattress, and flipped off the light. My dad might not be as easy to crack as Grandma Wiktoria's letters, but I was determined to do it. I would bring this family back together, one way or another.

6

The next morning, I woke up to a frosted wonderland. I checked the MLS to keep fresh on new listings, and then wandered about the house, still in my pajamas, wondering if I'd ever get any new clients interested in a house showing. I hadn't received any new messages in days.

I knew I should get dressed, so I'd be ready to go in case I got a call, but so far my morning had been spent on more pressing business of reheating the same mug of coffee over and over again because I kept getting distracted with chores needing to be done.

I was hanging up a load of laundry over the antique wooden drying rack—this cute old house had the most amazing claw tub but no electric dryer—when my phone dinged with an incoming text.

It was from Kari. **—Joe ate the potato salad and lived. I think he knew it was his last chance since I wouldn't be making it again for another year.**

I chuckled and wrote back, **—terrific!**

Then I grimaced. That wasn't the same news for poor Ian.

I walked through my bedroom and gathered clothing for the washing machine. As an old habit, I checked the pockets. There had been too many loads that I'd ruined with a pen back when I was in college.

The round metal piece in one of the pockets took me by surprise. The thing from Ian's house. I hadn't realized I'd stuffed it in my pants the day before.

Now that I had it out, I examined it closer. What was it?

It appeared to be the clasp of something. Yet it also looked like a screw-on top. It reminded me of one of the necklaces I had, but I hadn't seen a necklace in the bathroom when I'd cleaned it though. The thought crossed my mind that someone at Ian's house could have thrown it out and just missed the can. But they seemed to be the type who wore expensive jewelry. Wouldn't you want to repair it instead?

There was something odd about it besides the tiny threads. Studying it closer, I saw an 24k stamp which further supported my assumptions that whatever this belonged to was worth repairing.

Great. I needed to bring take back to Jasmine's house. What excuse could I use to go tromping in on her grief? I could bring a meal, but when I'd left, their fridge had already been stuffed from the party food.

Flowers? That's it! I could ask Uncle Chris if he'd want to contribute. Maybe the realty office could send some.

I jetted off a text to him with my question. Satisfied, I went back to stuffing the laundry into the machine. I hit start and brushed my hands together.

There. Another chore done.

My phone dinged with an alert. Uncle Chris was fast to respond today! I hummed as I clicked it open...a humming that quickly faded. My worst fear and suspicion had come true.

He wrote—**Coroner says it's murder.**

There was no time for a text back. I hit call.

"Hey," Uncle Chris answered, his voice heavy.

"Are you serious? How does he know? Are you okay?"

"Blood vessels burst under his skin. He also had blue fingernails. There's some other signs the coroner didn't go into, but it all points to acute poisoning. They are examining the stomach contents now."

Shocked, I reeled backward until I rested against the wall. I'd eaten that lunch! It could have been me!

"Uncle Chris, any one of us could have died!"

"I know. It's crazy. The detectives have returned to the house for samples of all the food and wine for testing. We should know more later."

I hung up the phone, my mind swirling in surrealness. It wasn't until I caught sight of the jewelry metal top on the counter that I realized my real reason in trying to get hold of Uncle Chris in the first place.

I picked it up and examined it again. Should I just chuck it? I mean, who would care in the light of Ian being murdered? This whole thing was bananas.

I dropped the jewelry piece into my purse, thinking I'd figure it out later.

Were they able to test all the food? They couldn't have tested Kari's potato salad. Kari and taken it home and Joe had eaten it. Of course, that meant it must have been safe. But what if it was a fluke? I scrambled to call her.

"Hello?" she answered, cheerily.

"Kari, don't let Joe eat any more of that potato salad! And for heaven's sake, keep the kids out of it!" I yelled into the phone, probably blasting out her eardrum. Panic had me in a frenzy.

"Stella? What's the matter?"

"It's Ian. Uncle Chris just called to say his death has been ruled as murder. They think he was poisoned."

Kari gasped. "Are you serious!" I could practically hear the implication clink into place. She gave a low moan. "I ate that food!"

"I know. It could have been any of us."

"My kids..." she whispered. The enormity of her statement hit like a ton of bricks. Her little boy and girl could have been left without a mother.

I swallowed hard. "I know."

"Who do they think did it?" she demanded, angrily. "Because there won't be a need to arrest them. I'm going to kill them, myself."

"Kari! Don't let anyone else hear you say that. I don't know who the police suspect. It could be any one of us."

"Any of us?" she squealed. "You mean I'm a suspect in a murder that almost knocked me off?"

It didn't make sense. Why would someone have done something that could have killed any one of us, including themselves? "Do you remember anyone avoiding any particular food item?" I asked.

"Well, there was Jasmine who didn't drink the wine."

I nodded, remembering that.

"Of course, Jasmine didn't seem to do much, other than push the food around on her plate," Kari continued.

"Celeste was the same way."

"Well, they are socialites. They might be on one diet or another. Everyone else seemed to enjoy their meal."

Everyone else had, including Ian.

My phone buzzed with an incoming text. It was from Uncle Chris. —**Call me ASAP**

7

"*U*h, Kari, I have to go. Uncle Chris wants to talk to me immediately."

"Oh, my gosh! What other horrible thing does he have to say? Go!" She hung up in a panic. I wasn't feeling much better as I called Uncle Chris.

"Stella, I forgot to tell you. You have a showing today," he said in a grief-stricken monotone.

I clutched the phone, my heart pounding. "What? That's it? You scared me with your text!"

"I'm sorry. The showing is in an hour. You need to get down to the Springfield Diner to meet them. It's actually the old buyers for Ian's place. Jennifer and Mark Clark. Jasmine has already stated she does not want to sell."

"Oh..."

"Yeah, so this couple is feeling a little desperate. I told them we could line up a couple of showings today. I'll send you the MLS numbers right now."

"Got it. I'm on my way."

A red notification in my email showed that the contact information for a Jennifer and Mark Clark, along with the house appointment that was scheduled had arrived. I shot them a text saying I was looking forward to meeting them and hurried to get dressed.

A SHORT TIME LATER, I parked in front of the Springfield Diner. The diner was built over fifty years ago and had been maintained to keep the same charm. White flower boxes filled with red geraniums—fake, I assume, considering it was winter —and a red-and-white awning completed the charm.

The Clarks were standing under the awning, trying to avoid a slushy pile of snow. Somewhere in their thirties, they were both bundled up with boots, hats, and scarves against the cold. Crimson cheeks and watery eyes greeted me as I walked up. Mark stuck out his hand for me to shake, while his wife, Jennifer, snuffled a red nose into the top of a zipped winter jacket.

"How are you two?" I asked, rubbing my hands briskly. My breath gusted in white clouds.

"Cold," chattered Jennifer. She appeared miserable. I knew I needed to get her out of the cold.

"Disappointed," added Mark.

"Oh, dear. Cold and disappointed. You want to grab a cup of coffee? Or just head straight to the showing?"

"If you don't mind, I want to get back into my warm car," Jennifer said. She turned and was already stiffly headed in that direction before I could respond.

"Okay, straight to the showing." I nodded to Mark. "You guys can follow me. I'm in that sedan over there."

With that, I hurried to my car. It was cold, so cold that the air burned the inside of my nose. Already, the temperature was lower than I'd usually seen it in Seattle. This was my first official winter out here, and the ol' thermometer was making me a little scared.

I climbed in and turned on the heat before plugging in the address to my phone's GPS. After it routed, I gave them a wave to let them know I was ready. They shot me a thumbs up, and we were off.

The bit of snow that had fallen the other day had mostly melted. Tall deciduous trees, their stark naked branches highlighted by the gray sky, flanked the road. Mingled around them were the evergreens. Along the fence lines, wild grass lay in wilted, rain-pounded waves.

I was looking forward to spring.

The map led across the valley into the next town, finally announcing we'd arrived at the front of a cute Colonial two-story. The driveway was empty.

I parked and climbed out as they were parking behind me. The air was quiet, the chilly temperature silencing what non-migrating birds clung to the branches and hid in hollows. Jennifer was still bundled in her jacket, not looking all that much warmer from when I last saw her.

"Beautiful place!" I puffed enthusiastically. She just looked longingly at the front door.

I trotted up the steps and located the lock box. Quickly, I punched in my code and retrieved the ice-cold key. The lock didn't give me any trouble, and we were soon inside.

Whew! It was warm inside, but the smell that hit was both unusual and strong—menthol. Like someone had waxed the furniture with vapor rub. My hand automatically went to my nose, unprofessional I know, but my eyes were watering.

"Well, that's interesting," I said, trying to cover.

"Stinky," said Mark, while Jennifer waved a hand in front of her face.

I closed the door behind us, and we slipped booties over our shoes. The house had an open floor plan with the dining room straight ahead of us. We walked over there.

"Oh, how nice. there's a connecting sunroom," I pointed out. At that moment, sunbeams cut through the many clouds and filtered through the sliding glass door, illuminating smear marks at the bottom as evidence to a very large dog.

"A little splash of window cleaner will clear that right up," I said, casually dismissing it. However, the marks put me on alert for more damage.

"We have a dog too, so it's okay. This house seems nice, Jennifer," Mark said, wrapping his arm around her waist.

Jennifer wrinkled her nose. "A bit dirty."

It was a tad more than 'a bit dirty', but that wasn't what was so off-putting. There was a feeling in the air that made the house seemed slightly unwelcoming, for lack of a better description.

We walked into the living room which practically pulsed from the sunlight bouncing off of lime green walls. Jennifer gasped, stopping dead in front of a wall of portraits laid out like a clock. It appeared really cute, and I couldn't understand her shocked expression until I walked closer and realized the pictures were of different sandwiches.

Uh... what kind of person has pictures of lunch meat on display?

"So, how are you doing with the homeowner's death?" I asked, trying to distract them. Too late, I realized I'd pulled out the big guns.

"Fine. I mean as well as can be expected," Jennifer said.

"I know that it's a shock for everybody, especially with an added blow for you guys because you thought you were buying the house."

"That house would've been perfect. But, of course, I understand why his wife is staying there." Mark answered.

"Well, I don't understand it. It was always a strange home for them." Jennifer flashed, crossing her arms. Her scowl set my teeth on edge.

Mark glanced at her with a tip of his head. Was that a subtle warning? She moved away from him.

He scratched the back of his neck. "You'll have to excuse my wife. It's kind of a sensitive subject."

Jennifer glared at her husband, obviously now feeling exposed and cornered at needing to explain herself.

Her husband wilted under the look and tried to cover. "We showed up at the house last week, a little unexpected," he said. "We were there to sign some papers, and I wanted to see about the possibility of building a dog run. We'd actually set up the time to meet the day before, but apparently, Ian and Jasmine had forgotten."

"So, you met them before?" I asked to clarify.

Jennifer rubbed her hands together and nodded.

"Yeah. We met them a few times." Mark continued. "Anyway, when we showed up on their porch, we could hear a lot of yelling, and we heard something break."

Here Jennifer interrupted. "Glass breaking. We didn't even have a chance to knock."

"Oh, my goodness!" I said. "What did you guys do?"

Mark glanced at Jennifer again and, this time, she gave a slight, permissive nod. "Well," he answered, "Ian was yelling that she needed to get with the program that he needed her support. Jasmine freaked out, saying that she could be pregnant, and this was a life sentence she was facing, and that it was up to him to fix this. Ian asked her how could she be pregnant. He'd gotten a vasectomy years ago. And she screamed at him that he was a liar."

My jaw dropped. Mark and Jennifer watched me, wide-eyed. They knew they had the goods.

"Did you tell any of this to the police?" I asked.

Mark shook his head as his wife answered. "Actually, we've never talked with the police. Do you think we should go to them?"

Did I think they should go to them? Yeah! Then I thought about Jasmine. She might be young and a little flighty, but did I really think she could be a killer?

My inner voice chided me. Of course. Wasn't the other half of a couple usually the main suspect?

I must have been frowning because Jennifer said, "Oh, I'm sorry. I didn't mean to upset you."

I shook my head, hoping to relieve her and get her talking some more. "No, you haven't at all. Other than the fact that the whole idea is upsetting."

Jennifer chewed on her thumbnail. "The reason why it upset me so much is that we've been trying so long. To have a baby." Her husband watched her with soft eyes. "So to hear her talk about it like that, it was hard. And then to have our dream house yanked away...."

My stomach plummeted. Oh, boy. I felt like the proverbial

bull in a china shop, dragging this poor woman into such a sensitive conversation.

I reached over and touched her elbow. "I'm so sorry. I didn't mean to bring up such a hard topic."

"It's okay. Everyone has their struggles." She shrugged nonchalantly, but I saw her lip tremble.

I nodded, wishing a hole would open up in the floor and swallow me up. We stood there for a moment. I really had no idea how to continue.

Luckily, her husband saved the day. Standing with his hands on his hips, facing the wall, he blurted out, "This clock is a bunch of bologna."

We all laughed, mostly with relief. "Mark, you're so corny!" Jennifer said, leaning into him. He wrapped his arm around her shoulder and pulled her in tight for a kiss on the head.

We wandered through the bedrooms—six of them, all stuffed with odd furniture. One room was filled with big, round Papasan chairs. Another was a quilting room, set up with a permanent built-in table and quilt stretcher.

The master bedroom was nice, with a window seat and a five-piece en-suite bathroom. It was here that I discovered where the dog slept. A giant cedar pillow lay on the floor, accompanied by black marks on the wall.

As I followed the Clark's, I thought about Jasmine possibly being pregnant. But the other shocker was that Jasmine insisted it was a life sentence they were facing. Was she talking metaphorically about how a child was a lifetime commitment?

Or was she referring to actual jail time?

Jennifer had paused outside a linen closet.

"What's that in there?" she asked, her voice tinged with concern.

I glanced inside. There was another door in the back of the closet. I reached in and tried to open it but it was stuck fast.

Grunting, I tried the door again, as well as casually trying to approach the conversation one more time. "You know, I think you should consider talking to the police about your experience. It might be nothing, but with it so close to Ian's death, you never know." I gave up on the door. It wasn't going to budge. I hoped I had better luck convincing Jennifer.

She blanched and licked her bottom lip nervously.

I quickly reassured, "You aren't accusing anyone. Jasmine and Ian could have been fighting over something that involved the real killer. Maybe it was a blackmail letter or something, and Jasmine hasn't shared it out of her own fear."

That line of reasoning seemed to convince her. She glanced

at her husband who gave a firm bob of his head. Her lips pressed together resolutely. "Right. We'll stop at the station right after this."

I smiled and shut the linen closet door. "Good for you. So, are we done here, then?"

Jennifer glanced up at the ceiling where a trail of cobwebs shivered in the draft. "Yes, we're done."

Her husband laughed. "I swear we could just clean this all up."

"You can't clean up a door that leads to nowhere." She pointed to the closet. "Uncle Motes could live in there."

"Uncle Motes?" I asked.

Her husband chuckled some more. "Her childhood boogyman that her cousins used to scare her with."

"Shut up!" she squealed. "I saw him, I swear. A big shadowy man with a hat. He used to lurk at my grandparent's house in the basement."

I joined their giggles as I walked them to the front door. Jennifer was still jabbering away about it as they headed to their car.

But when I turned around to go back through the house to make sure everything was secure, the story didn't seem as funny. The sun was back to hiding behind the clouds and a pallor of gray gloom filled the rooms. I hurried through them to check the back door, trying to ignore the squeaking boards and dark shadows. I was just testing the back door knob when a subtle gust of cold air drifted down my neck. Just like last time, I felt I was being watched.

Slowly, I turned.

The door to the linen closet had swung open. I reached to shut it when I realized the door in the back of the closet, the one that had been jammed shut, was open as well. Cobwebs drifted from around the frame with the cold air draft. I slammed the linen closet door shut and ran back to the front door. The owners could close the other one. I was out of there, like a pig being called to dinner.

Once outside on the porch, I had to laugh at myself. I was being so ridiculous. Still, I couldn't deny my hands were trembling. I hated unexplainable things.

I didn't have much more time to think about it. As I waved goodbye to Jennifer and Mark and hurried to my car, my phone rang.

8

The phone call was from Kari. As I started the car, her voice piped through the speakers, "Have you heard?"

"Heard what?" I asked, pulling out onto the road.

"The coroner said he found a bunch of undigested antacids in Ian's stomach. He must have taken them just minutes before he was murdered."

I remember the bottle on the counter. I knew they somehow had been important!

"Do you think there's an explanation why? Maybe it was the stress from his phone call. Or all of us being there?"

"I think it was the poison. It proves he must have eaten something that killed him," Kari answered adamantly.

I wasn't sure it had been the food. I now suspected the wine the neighbor brought over. There was that glass that I'd dumped that had a sour scent. I remembered Ian had taken a huge swig just before he'd left the table. And it was as he swallowed that he'd grimaced. I didn't think Gordon had shared it with anyone else. I remember Jasmine had covered her own glass.

That theory just didn't make sense though. Ian and Jasmine were moving, so Gordon wouldn't be dealing with them much longer. Besides, why would you kill your neighbor over Christmas lights or leaving trash cans out?

I was about to say something when Kari chimed in again. "By the way, I meant to tell you. Joe and I want to have you over for dinner."

Well, that came out of left field and immediately, I was suspicious. Not because she was inviting me, but people don't go out of their way to bring up their spouse in the invitation to single friends unless something was afoot.

"Really. And why is that?" I came straight to the point.

"Stella! Honestly. Can't we just be a couple of close friends who want to have a nice dinner together?"

"Mmhmm," I said, sarcasm-heavy.

There was a pause, and then she gave in. "Fine. Joe has a friend we really want you to meet. He's a nice guy and—"

"I knew it!"

"Stella! Seriously, you hardly ever leave the house. You're practically a cave creature. It would be good to get out and make friends. Thomas is a nice guy. He just got out of a relationship and—"

"That means he has a lot of baggage."

"It means he needs to meet a nice person as well. So, come to dinner. Help restore his faith in humanity. Besides, I really think you two will really hit it off. I promise. It'll be a nice dinner. We're barbecuing steak."

I huffed but finally said all right. Kari was a persuasive person. And I knew I was no match for her. She confirmed the plans for the weekend and then hung up.

As I drove to the office, a million thoughts tumbled through my mind. Was it because Jasmine was pregnant that she refused the wine? And, was it even possible to slip poison into a corked bottle? Why had Ian taken the antacids? Stress?

There was also that curious phone call Ian had been on when he first walked into the house. Didn't he accuse that person of extortion?

I wondered if the police knew about the phone call. If Jasmine was somehow guilty, would she have mentioned it to them? Would anyone? I know I didn't.

No one was at the realty when I arrived. I walked inside and threw my keys on my desk, only to be confronted with a giant note. Well, the note was normal paper size, but the writing, scrawled in Uncle Chris's chicken scratch, could have been read across the room.

"Stella! It needs to be signed today."

The note was lying on a folder. I opened it and saw some forms that the Clark's had signed to dissolve the contract. All that was needed was a signature from Jasmine. I wrinkled my nose and groaned.

Why hadn't he brought it to Jasmine to sign himself? He's friends with her. I was going to be like the Abominable Snowman stomping all over the poor woman's grief.

A tiny voice added... unless she's guilty.

I rolled my eyes. I just couldn't see how that young woman would have been capable of such cold-blooded murder, and with all of us there. Technically, we were each other's alibis.

I picked up the phone as dread settled in the pit of my stomach. I mean, the guy wasn't even buried yet. Still, the forms had to be signed by today.

I sighed and scrolled for Jasmine's number. Figuratively crossing my fingers, I pushed send, hoping I wasn't going to get a crying widow on the other end.

"Hello?" Jasmine answered. Her voice so soft, I couldn't get a read on her emotional state.

"Jasmine? It's Stella from Flamingo Realty. How are you?"

"Oh," she sniffed. "I've been better."

"I'm so sorry," I said, cringing. That had been a stupid question to ask.

"It's okay. I miss him. The doctor has me on some amazing pills to help me stay calm though. I'm so relaxed now, I could do brain surgery."

That kind of took me off guard. Can you take a prescription like that when you're pregnant? Maybe Jennifer misheard. I shook my head. That wasn't possible, not with it hitting so close to home for the Clarks. The medication was either safe, or she wasn't pregnant. Either way, it gave me no new information.

I glanced at the papers and tried to reel myself in to the business at hand. "I'm glad the doctor gave you something that helps. I really hate to bother you, but is there any way I could stop by for a minute?"

"Sure. What's going on?"

"I just have one more thing for you to sign to release everyone from the contract."

She laughed. "Join the club. Everyone has something for me to do. The funeral home, the coroner, the insurance company. It's been a deluge of requests around here."

"I'm so sorry. I promise I'll make it quick."

"It's fine. We need to get it done and, after all, life goes on. I'm free this afternoon."

"Okay. I'll see you soon."

I hung up and gathered my things. Why did I feel so icky?

A GREEK GYRO and fries and an hour later, I pulled into Jasmine Stuber's driveway. There was a red car already there, along with a white Hummer. I popped a mint into my mouth and then gathered the papers. That little inner voice tried to chime in and accuse me of delaying, but I ignored it and slammed the car door instead. Taking a deep breath, I walked up to the porch.

Jasmine answered, looking chic in a simple beige shirt, pencil skirt and a pearl necklace. I was surprised to see her so put-together but remembered the doctor had her somewhat sedated.

"Stella," she said with a smile. She touched my arm, surprising me. We were practically strangers, but she was acting like I was an old friend that she hadn't seen in a long time. "Come in. Celeste is already here."

I remembered Celeste. Jasmine's cousin.

She led me through the house into the kitchen, which was filled with an array of white arrangements of flowers. Although lovely, I couldn't see how comforting they would be. These flowers had a funeral look about them, both stiff and formal.

Her home smelled amazing thought. I sniffed deeply and let out a contented hum. I saw steam rising from a little figurine on a buffet in the living room.

She pointed to it and said, "That's my diffuser. I have stress relief oil going right now."

"It smells wonderful," I said. "Does it really take stress away? I might need a gallon."

She laughed, high and tinkling, taking me off guard. "Not as well as this does," she said, producing a prescription bottle from her hidden pocket.

I wondered if maybe she should have her prescription lowered. She seemed awfully jovial for what she'd just gone through.

We walked down the long hallway and into the kitchen.

Celeste stood from the bar stool when I entered. She wore a leather jacket and designer jeans, the tips of a pair of boots peeping out from the long cuffs. Her blonde hair was slicked back in a style that appeared slightly wet.

"Hello, Celeste." I bobbed my head in her direction.

"Nice to see you again, Stella," she coolly acknowledged. She perched back on the bar stool where a cup sat before her.

"Can I get you some coffee?" Jasmine asked me.

I shuffled through my purse for a pen. "No, I don't want to be a bother." I set the paper on the counter. "There's just one little signature needed, and a couple of initials." I pointed to the highlighted line.

Celeste leaned over in a cloud of perfume. "What's this?"

"Oh, just something I need to sign to get out of the contract," Jasmine answered.

"So, you're keeping your house after all." Celeste stared at Jasmine and I swear some sort of communication flashed between their eyes.

But Jasmine didn't let on if there was a deeper meaning to Celeste's statement. She shrugged casually and accepted my pen. "Until I know better what I'm going to do, it's best for me to stay here. My body's having a hard time with the stress."

I noticed a bottle of antacids on the counter, the same ones I'd tucked to one side on the day of the party. "Is your stomach acting up? I hope you're feeling okay."

She quickly scribbled where I pointed and then followed my gaze. She shook her head. "No, those are... were Ian's. He had indigestion something terrible. He was on several prescriptions for it. Finally, we tried essential oils. It was the first thing that seemed to help."

I was surprised. I'd never heard of using oil before for heartburn. "Did he eat them?" Maybe that was the cause of his stomach upset at the party.

"No, it came in a roller ball. Celeste made it for him. You rub it on your skin, and it absorbs to help balance out the heartburn. Here, look at the one she made me." At that, she opened a drawer and rummaged through it. Not finding what she wanted, she dug into her purse. With a hum of satisfaction, she brought out a little glass bottle. She unscrewed the black top to reveal a metal roller ball.

"Smell it," Jasmine said. "This one helps with anxiety."

I sniffed it. The musky mixture of sandalwood and something else was appealing.

"Can't you just feel your worries draining away?" Jasmine asked.

I nodded. The muscles in my neck did seem more relaxed. "That's amazing." Carefully, I screwed on the cap and handed it back.

"You can get the oils down at Heritage Dispensary. This is my own special blend." Jasmine glanced at her cousin. "Well, Celeste's special blend. They have all styles. Roller balls, tinctures, necklace lockets, bracelets, and concentrate. There are soap, lotions, body oils. I could get lost in there all day."

"Wow! I had no idea." It did make me wonder. I understood why Jasmine would use a doctor's prescription now, in light of Ian's murder. But she was using the stress and anxiety oils before his death. What had been going on that kept her so agitated?

That agitation seemed to have disappeared as she smiled at me. "I can get you one if you want. I have lots. Celeste keeps me supplied."

Celeste leaned forward on the stool. "It's a passion. It's amazing how oils can bring balance to the system. Of course, not all oils are the same. It can be a little overwhelming. If you have any questions or want an education, let me know."

"She's obsessed. But they do work, so I give her that. And she has such a talent at making blends."

They were both so enthusiastic it was hard not to smile. "I'll have to check that dispensary out. Heritage, you say?"

Jasmine tucked a fallen blonde wisp behind her ear. "They have classes, too. I was thinking of taking one to make my own perfume. The owner is super nice."

I gathered the papers back into the manila folder. "I'll be sure to stop by there one day when I'm in town. And, thank you for doing this, Jasmine. Again, I'm sorry. I'll get out of your hair, now."

"Oh, it's fine. You're not in my hair," she reassured me. "The distraction is actually nice." Her bottom lip trembled. "Otherwise, I'm left to my own thoughts. It feels like a nightmare that keeps getting worse and worse. And the latest news... I just can't believe... can't believe he was murdered."

"Shh." Celeste put an arm around her and pulled her close like she was a little girl.

My heart dropped to see her crying. I'd rather face a forest fire than this poor woman's grief. I had no idea what to do.

"Who would have done something like that, Celeste? Who?" Jasmine sobbed into her cousin's shoulder.

"I'm not sure, sweetheart. But we'll find him."

Jasmine leaned away and wiped her cheeks. Her spiky eyelashes still had managed not to smudge. She bit her lip, appearing young and fragile. "Who do you think could have done it, Stella?"

I definitely wasn't expecting that question to pop out of her mouth. But it seemed like the perfect opportunity to ask one of my own. "Jasmine, Ian was yelling at someone on the phone when he came in that day. Do you remember? Do you have any idea who he was arguing with?"

"Arguing with?" she looked confused.

"Yes. Remember, we were all hiding, and he came in sounding upset on the phone. I was just curious if you ever tracked that down."

"Oh," she nodded.

"Wasn't that his brother?" Celeste suggested.

"That's right! He said his brother was teasing him about going to St. John's instead of his parent's party."

"Is there any way you could check that? Maybe look over his phone records just to be sure." I suggested, my stomach sinking for being so pushy.

"I guess I could find out," she answered, a little dubious. Her thin hands twisted together.

"Sure, it would be easy," Celeste said. "It could be important, you never know."

My face was hot. I'd used up all my time, and I needed to get out of there. "I'm sorry to bother you with that. I just was curious."

"Oh, no bother at all. It's a good point. It might be nice for me to find out for myself," she said.

I reached into my purse for my keys and felt the piece of jewelry. "I almost forgot. When I was cleaning up, I found this the other day."

Jasmine took it from me and examined it. Her face appeared confused.

"I'm sorry I took it with me. I got distracted about something and forgot about that," I explained.

"I have no idea who it belongs to. It looks like it's a part of a necklace."

"I found it in the bathroom, the one where Ian..." I paused, not sure how to continue.

Celeste took a turn looking at it and the handed it back. "It's not mine, either."

I dropped it back in my purse. The conversation great stale, and the air had that heavy prickliness of me overstaying my welcome.

For an excuse to leave, I peeked at my phone. "Oh, shoot. I'm sorry, I'm running late. Jasmine, if there is anything I can do for you, anything at all, please don't hesitate to call us at the office. I apologize again for the intrusion." With a dip of my head, I hurried from the kitchen and out to my car.

9

*A*t the first stop sign leaving Jasmine's house, I picked up the phone again. I wasn't really late anywhere, but the jewelry piece was suddenly making me worried. Call it a hunch, but I felt pressed to get this piece out of my hands. After all, I did find it in the bathroom that Ian had died in. I dialed the police station and sent the call through my car's microphone.

"Is Officer Daniels available?" I asked when the phone was answered. "He's working on a case. Ian Stuber's death. I found something that might be a clue."

I was told he was out on his shift and would be happy to meet me outside the Post Office.

Very well. I headed into Brookfield and drove through

Darcy's Doughnuts for an Americano—whimpering slightly at the scent of freshly glazed cream-puffs—and then on to the Post Office. Like nearly everything else in town, it was the original founding building with brick edifices and columns carefully preserved. A golden decal of an eagle decorated the front door. Through the glass, I could see the dark head of Jan as she walked by, carrying a stack of boxes.

Jan was the postmaster who knew everything about everybody. I took a sip of coffee and watched her move about the office like a busy bee. She disappeared in the back, only to reappear a moment later with a broom in her hand. She was a hard worker and seemed motivated to prove it. I knew how she feared retirement.

A police car pulled in behind me. I immediately stiffened when I realized it was not Officer Daniels, but his partner, Officer Carlson behind the wheel. His bald head was hidden under his police cap, but I'd recognize him anywhere. With the narrowing of his eyes and the way the lines carved around his lips, he wore a scowl that could have made Al Capone shiver.

What was his problem? I climbed out of my car and saw that Jan's sweeping activity had stalled as she watched. Terrific. Her nose was practically pressed against the glass like Gladys Kravitz from Bewitched. She was probably taking notes, I was sure, and it wouldn't be long now before the entire town knew I was meeting with the police. In fact, by the time the news got back to me, I bet the story would be that I was in handcuffs, being carted off to the pokey.

Of course, by Officer Carlson's glower, that might not be out of the realm of possibility.

"Hi, Officer Carlson," I said, walking back to him.

He eased one foot to step onto the curb. "Hollywood," he said with a nod.

He was never going to let that go, was he? I'd roll my eyes, but like I said, he looked like he was in a mood. Still, I had to defend myself. "It's Washington, remember? The Northwest."

His eyebrows slanted upward like he didn't care. "You still seem like Hollywood to me. Now, what is it you have that's so important?"

I held out the metal piece of jewelry. "I stumbled across this in the bathroom. You know, the one Ian was discovered in. I couldn't find out who it belonged to so I figured I better hand it to you."

He pulled out a clear plastic bag, making the muscles under his shirt flex, and held it open with a heavy sigh. I dropped it in and he lifted it to examine it. Like up, up. The guy was well over a foot taller than me. "Looks nice and pawed on.

What have you been doing? Carrying this thing in a vaseline jar?"

"Sorry." I cringed. "I never even thought about trying to preserve fingerprints until later." My cheeks heated under the melting glare of the cop. But how was I supposed to know it could be a clue? At the time I found it, Ian appeared to have died from a heart attack. Heck, I was trying to do a good deed by tidying things up so there weren't any party remnants for the grieving widow.

"So let me guess. You tried to do some detecting into who this belongs to. How exactly did you do that?" he asked.

Feeling like a deer in headlights under his stern expression, I swallowed. "I asked both Jasmine and Celeste if it was theirs."

"And what did they say?" he seemed interested, holding the bag up again.

"They both denied that it belonged to them."

"Are you saying that you actually handed it over to them to examine?"

"Yeah. They both got a good look," I reassured him.

Shaking his head, he twisted the bag closed as the frown lines around his lips creased deeper than the wrinkles in the plastic.

"What?" I finally asked.

"Oh, nothing," he said, pursing his lips sarcastically. "It's just that we don't usually tell our suspects about our evidence, let alone offer them a chance to handle it."

My jaw dropped. "Jasmine really is a suspect?" I finally whispered.

"What would you call a woman who stands to inherit a five million dollar life insurance policy?" he asked.

I was shocked. "Was it poison?" I asked, remembering what Uncle Chris said.

He casually lifted a shoulder, clearly not interested in sharing information. "I'm not here to confirm nor deny, but usually the common sense answer is the right one. Anyway, we're aiming to find out. It's kind of what the detecting business is. Weirdly, what we are trained for." His gaze flicked at me, and the corner of his lip lifted, revealing a dimple.

I ignored the jab. "I might have another clue. On the day of the party, while we were all hiding, Ian was yelling at someone on the phone when he first came in. Something about extortion. And he was going to kill them."

Officer Carlson's dark eyes narrowed. He set the bag on the back of my car and pulled out a pad. "And no one at the scene thought to tell us this?"

"I don't think we realized it could be important."

"What else was said during the phone call?"

I quickly described what I remembered. "Ian later told us it was his brother. In fact, I just asked Jasmine to find out for sure since it might be important. She said she would check the phone records to confirm it."

"We'll get those records checked," he growled, as his gaze swept across what he'd been writing.

"So, do you have any suspects besides Jasmine?" I asked.

"At this point, we are digging into anyone who may have had a motive."

"And you have a few?"

He arched his eyebrow, and his eye sparkled like he was trying not to laugh. "Maybe a few. Anyone ever told you that you ask a lot of questions, Hollywood?"

I bit my lip, struggling not to roll my eyes, reminding myself that I needed to tread lightly with him. "Sorry. I just can't believe that one of us there had to have done it. It's really shocking."

"And what about you? Have you ever met Ian Stuber before?"

Oh, great. Was he just poking at me to punish me for

handling the jewelry? Or was I really someone they were suspicious about?

"Just as a client. The Flamingo Realty was selling his house. He was Uncle Chris's old friend."

"Yeah, an old friend and racing buddy." He glanced back at his paper. "It seems there was bad blood between them at one time."

A chill ran down my back. Was he accusing Uncle Chris of something? "I think it was normal that most race car drivers experienced animosity at one time or another."

His eyebrow lifted. "You'd describe it as animosity?" He quickly scribbled some more.

What? No! "What I mean is that it was all in the competitive spirit of the racetrack."

He nodded. "They were competitive, huh? So it mustn't have felt too good when Ian won the last three races that your Uncle Chris was in. In fact, they were the last races your Uncle ever competed in."

Whoa. This guy knew a lot more than I'd given him credit for. "That was years ago. They've been good friends ever since, like old fraternity brothers."

He snapped his notebook shut. "Thank you for your time and for giving us the clue. If you think of anything else, let us know. I'm always here, digging around." He smiled, and it scared me. With a dip of his head, he stalked away.

As he climbed in his car, I glanced over at the Post Office. There was my reflection in the window, with my mouth still hanging open. I shut it, realizing how it must look, a big ol' fish gasping for air on the sidewalk. It was a moment later when I realized that Jan was on the other side of the glass. She had the phone to ear and was talking a mile a minute. When she realized she'd been caught, she'd grabbed her broom and hurried out of sight.

10

My thoughts were overtaking me by the time I arrived home. They were coming so fast, I could hardly remember which way was up anymore. From Officer Carlson's jabbing questions, to Celeste asking about my mom, to Uncle Chris's face of grief.

Maybe it was his grief that was triggering all of this confusion. I sat in the car, too overwhelmed to even get out. The feeling was suffocation. I leaned my head to rest on my hands clutching the top of the steering wheel. I needed something... someone. It reminded me of another time I had the same need.

When I was younger, I dreamed of being a ballerina. I was nine and hadn't known that all real ballerinas had already been training for five plus years by my age. With crazy stars in my eyes, I'd tried out for the Pacific Northwest Ballet Nutcracker, thinking it was like a school play and that I would learn as I went. There were ninety roles available for children, everything from angels, to soldiers, dancing girls, to mice. The audition hall was filled with kids.

I noticed the difference between them and myself right away. While I was giggling with excitement, they were stretching, faces serious. Arms posed, toes pointed. When I tried to talk to them, they'd turn their faces in the other direction.

I didn't even make it for a dancing candy cane. The whole experience was more than embarrassing, with one of the directors finally approaching me (with stressed eyes and an overly-patient face) to advise me that I take some lessons and maybe try again in a few years.

Of course, he'd known that I'd never come back. I did actually take a few lessons, a giant fifth grader clumsily looming over the tops of the little kids in that beginner class. It was especially stinging and awkward because even those kids had been able to follow the dance moves better than I had.

At my last lesson, I'd gone to the car wanting to cry. Craving a mom to talk with. Instead, there was Dad, a real 'pull yourself up by your bootstraps,' and 'never give up on something you've committed to doing' kind of guy."

I didn't know how to tell him I didn't want to go back. As it turned out, I hadn't needed to. Apparently, the teacher had had a little talk with Dad while I was waiting in the car.

Dad never brought it up again. The next week, when it was time for my dance lesson, Dad sat in his favorite spot on the couch and turned on his favorite cop show. I'd watched from the doorway with my ballet slippers and my jacket. When he didn't move, I snuck back into my room and hid the slippers under my mattress. And I'd cried, needing... something. The same need I had right now.

I never took the slippers out again. In fact, they probably were still stuffed between the mattresses. Dad never asked. I don't think he knew how to deal with a daughter, in some ways. Especially how to deal with the emotions of a broken dream.

As I thought about that now, I realized then my mom must have had dreams as well.

What had she dreamed of? This woman who I barely remember. Surely, she didn't dream of having a daughter and then never seeing her again. Did she? What had happened to her?

I drummed my fingers against the steering wheel as the feeling grew. What had I done to deal with all of this before? Was it the running? Had it helped me that much?

I used to run. Not in the way that many people did. I definitely didn't do it for exercise, but for sport. I was insanely proud of my record time and had developed a disgusting habit of slipping it into conversations with a little humble-bragging. That had been another dream of mine, to one day try out for the Olympics.

All that ended in college when I came up against people who'd wiped the floor with my best times. I'd given up the sport and, to be honest, I hadn't run again. We're looking at nearly ten years here.

I don't know why I quit. Pride, I guess. The utter humiliation to lose race after race after being the all-star for my school. The fear of facing my father.

Slowly, something was occurring to me. Here I am trying to dig out my identity from Dad's expectations, and even my own self-imposed rules. And thinking about childhood dreams made me realize that, yes, I had been addicted to the competition and the winning highs. To my dad's approval.

But, at the heart of it, there was a real love for running. Something about the way my feet hit the ground rhythmically, my heart and breaths coming in controlled gasps, well there was an indescribable soothingness about it all. Probably that endorphin stuff. I realize now that it had helped me through those angsty teenage years, even though the wins blew up my head and ego.

Running had been a space in time where I could think.

You'd think I have lots of space and time at the moment, rattling around in this old house by myself. I climbed out of the car, feeling drained and tired.

The truth was, I was starting to feel stagnant. Somehow, since I'd moved back, I'd slumped into a habit where I was only leaving the house for work. In fact, if I was being honest, Ian's party had been the first time I'd been out in a while. That couldn't be healthy. Heck, at work I'd become some morphed version of super realtor Stella, instead of the authentic person I was trying to figure out. Had I substituted my uncle for my dad, trying to make him proud?

I walked into the house and somehow ended up at my bedroom closet. On the floor was a sad pair of tennis shoes. I picked one up. It was a little worn, but the arch support inside was still okay. The wear-and-tear was really only on the outside.

My heart thumped with anticipation... excitement. Yeah, I was ready to run again. I needed to quit doing things to make someone else proud. I needed to figure out what makes me happy, and do it, even if it means I'm not the best.

I laced up the shoes, found my old gray college sweatshirt and pulled it on with a smile. It was cold outside, but I knew I'd warm up pretty quick. I walked outside and eyed the road. The frost was heavy on the ground and my breath puffed in white dragon clouds. I was doing what I wanted. Just to make me happy.

Wow. It made me feel alive.

Okay, first, stretch. After the first hamstring stretch, I slipped into muscle memory. Calves, quads. I shook out my legs.

It was time.

Now, which way? There was a creek down somewhere past the neighbor's field. I'd seen the dark smudge of bushes outlining it when I'd driven up to the house. From that direction, I could hear the croak of frogs.

I started jogging and gasped as unexpected emotions exploded inside of me. Suddenly, I was brought back to the shame of the loss at my last college race—was that the last time I ran?—when I finally accepted that I was no one special. My feet hit the ground even as my cheeks heated.

I realized now how much of my identity and value rested on me having a label. To be known by the label. Honor roll, track star, entrepreneur, go-getter, motivated.

And when I couldn't achieve it, it nearly crushed me. Again and again. So I'd try harder. Harder to have value.

It occurred to me, I'd never told Dad that I'd quit track. He would have freaked out. My breath came out in frosty clouds as I remembered. In his eyes, an O'Neil never quits.

I wondered if he thought me moving back to Pennsylvania was quitting.

The rhythmic smacks of my shoes against the road had a calming effect. I enjoyed this. How had I forgotten?

And what had brought back this stifling feeling so strongly?

Ian's death. That's what it was. He woke up that morning with plans and by that afternoon, his life was over. He thought he had time still to achieve his hopes and dreams.

I didn't want to miss out on what was important to me because of fear that my dad would think I was failing. That's why I'd moved out here. Wasn't it? Wasn't it?

Anger fueled my steps, and I pounded my feet harder on the road, eating up the asphalt. All right, so I got a little complacent since taking the big plunge to move out here. I was ready now. Ready to fight for what I wanted.

And right now, I wanted to know more about my mother.

Was her hair the same color as mine? Did I look like her? Did she die, or was she still out there... somewhere?

Was it possible that I'd already run into her? Had she spied on me while growing up, like my FBI retired Grandfather admitted to doing? Or did she truly just walk away, not caring anymore about the little girl she'd left behind? And how had I locked her memory up so tight that I'd never tried to answer these before?

I knew why. Because I still had one identity that I didn't want to give up. Being loyal to my dad.

My foot caught on a patch of ice, and I tumbled across the icy pavement. A yelp escaped out of me in the whoosh of breath. I lay there, crying, on the cold ground.

My tears weren't from pain. Falling was a welcome relief to finally let them free. I hugged my knees and cried.

For her.

For me.

For my dad.

Then I examined my ankles, but they were fine. My hand had a few scrapes from landing. Wincing, I stood and started to limp home. But, despite the physical pain, I was feeling better.

As I looked down the long, lonely road, I noticed a black truck. It looked mean, with a bulky grill, like teeth, and a silver frame around the license plate that glinted in the light. The vehicle had stopped dead smack right in the middle of the road.

Just as if the driver were watching me.

11

The truck rumbled, not moving.

A chill trickled up my arms, and not from the cold temperature. He'd been coming up like that behind me while I was running. My brain tried to come up with a rational explanation. Was he looking for something? Trying to map somewhere?

Any of those might have worked, but I could see the driver wasn't moving. He sat like a statue, staring ahead.

Straight at me.

That's weird. Where did he come from and what the heck is he doing? I tested my ankle and started to jog again, feeling the need to get home.

The gravel and ice crunched under my feet. As I ran, I realized how isolated I was. This road was long. There was nothing but flat fields on both sides, tilled-over and snow-covered at the moment, with a dark hedge of trees in the distance.

The truck's engine continued to idle, the driver still watching me. I tried to see inside the windshield, but the reflection was too strong to make out details.

It was at that moment I realized my house was too far away. I made a crazy decision and turned down the driveway I'd passed every day since I'd moved there. I'd always wondered who'd lived in this little frame house that sat all summer long like a white postage stamp on a green envelope of waving wheat that surrounded it. But today, I was looking for a little neighborly support.

I ran down the driveway, my heart pounding. The black truck revved its engine. With a tight maneuver, it started to turn around. Smoke plumed from its exhaust as the driver stomped on the gas, making the tires spit up gravel and slush.

I felt a little foolish. Maybe he'd just stopped to read a map. Stopping in the middle of the road was odd, but you never knew. Still, I wasn't taking any chances. This was as good of a time as any to meet my neighbor.

I knocked on the door.

A woman, somewhere in her late sixties, came out to the porch. She had on a heavy fisherman's sweater and thick jeans.

"I'm sorry," I heaved. "This is so odd, but I was out here running, and there was this truck on the road that kind of creeped me out."

"Oh, my heavens!" she exclaimed craning her head to stare down the road. The truck had managed to complete the tight turn and was already nearly at the T in the road. With a screech of his tires, he disappeared.

"Well, isn't that—she paused, looking confused. "Dang it. I can't remember his name. He lives around here somewhere. Well, why don't you come in for a glass of water."

She led me into her kitchen, my heart thumping since I hadn't had time to cool down. I hoped she'd remember who the person in the truck was.

Her movements were slow, and it appeared that her joints hurt. With a small muffled sigh, she got down a glass cup—prism cut, with a heavy bottom—and filled it at the sink, the whole time with her brow puckered in thought.

"I'm Stella O'Neil," I volunteered. "I live in the house up the street."

"Right!" She smiled, appearing relieved. She brushed back a

graying wisp that had fallen into her face. "The old Crawford's house?"

"Yes," I nodded.

Unexpectedly, the back door flew open with a bang. I jumped and tried to recover. A man walked in, wearing ripped jeans and an olive green t-shirt. A t-shirt that fit quite nicely, I noted. Both were covered in smears of black grease. He stared at me in surprise. Green eyes too, matched his shirt. I quickly took a sip of water.

"Richie, this is our neighbor." The woman looked confused again.

"Stella," I offered.

He nodded, dark eyebrows raising, and held out a hand, before flushing when he realized how dirty it was. His hair was long as well, brushing the edge of his collar. "I guess I won't shake. I'm working on the old beast. The car, I mean."

"She's our neighbor," the woman said proudly.

"That's great, Ma," he said. "You've been a good hostess, I see."

She turned bright eyes toward me. "Since you're here, would you like to see my dolls?"

It was then that I realized the poor woman had some senility issues. I glanced at Richie, who seemed embarrassed. He walked to the sink to wash his hands. "She doesn't want to look at your dolls, Ma."

The woman's face fell in the most heart-breaking way.

"Of course," I rushed to answer. "I'd love to see them. I love dolls."

Her face lit up and she walked to the entrance of another room. "Come just this way," she beckoned.

I walked through the doorway and into the living room. Immediately, I was slapped in the face with the fact that I didn't love dolls nearly as much as I'd just professed.

Walls, shelves, and display cases were filled with the smiling toys. Some dolls stared with tipped heads, some had eyes that could open and close, but something wonky had happened, and their eyelids were uneven in a half wink. But they all felt like they were staring straight through me. Like 'don't turn your back on them' staring.

I rubbed my arm. "Wow! These are nice. You've been collecting for a while?"

"Oh, yes. This one is from my childhood." She pointed to a doll with worn nubs for hair. "And that one over there Richie got me for Christmas." This was a doll in a white princess gown, covered in glitter. The woman's face shone with pride.

"That was a sweet gift," I said. And I meant it.

We talked for a while, as she pointed out her favorites. Richie stood uneasily at the doorway until I finally said I needed to go. She seemed disappointed, so I promised I'd come back for a visit. Satisfied, with that promise, I left her fluffing one of the doll's ballgown.

Richie walked with me out onto the porch. He wore cowboy boots that looked like they'd seen better times. "Thank you for that," he said, dipping his head in the direction of his mother. "She loves to have company."

"Oh, any time," I said. And I meant it.

"She's kind of been having a rough time ever since Dad died. It's why I work from home. Just to keep an eye on things. She's doing good but I like to be around in case she needs me."

"Aww, that's very sweet. I'm sure you are a great help to her."

"I try." He shrugged and then smoothed his dark hair off his forehead. His hand washing skills hadn't finished the job and he left a mark of grease on his skin.

"What is it you do?" I asked.

"I'm a mechanic. I have my own shop in town, but now I work out back by the barn. It's kind of crazy, and definitely not as convenient as the shop in town, but, like I said, I moved things."

We chatted some more and then I realized with a blush that I'd eaten more than enough of his time. I said goodbye and headed home.

After I left, I realized I still didn't know his mom's name. Slowly, I jogged down the road. My ankles were fine, but I didn't want to push it.

I was thinking about that when I noticed tire tracks outside my driveway. I'd completely forgotten about the black truck. Who had been watching me?

12

I walked up the creaking stairs of my porch and into my house, mentally yelling at myself for not locking the door. I didn't want to be alone while I searched the house, so I called Uncle Chris.

"Yellow?" answered my uncle, answering in his usually goofy way.

"Hey, Uncle Chris." I racked my brain for an excuse to call. "Uh, just wanted to check in." I rolled my eyes and opened the closet door. Nothing there.

"Well, you have good timing. I just got word that they identified the poison that killed Ian. It's called Trogia Venenata. Little White. A fungus. It's extremely rare and in fact, not around here at all. The coroner isn't sure how Ian got into contact with it." Uncle Chris paused, and I could almost picture him rubbing his neck the way that he did when he was perplexed.

I wonder if Officer Carlson knew that, and that's why he was being so cagey. "How did you find out?" I asked, heaving a little as I climbed down to peer under the bed.

"I have my ways."

"So they don't think he ate it?" I asked to clarify, dusting myself off.

"No. It came in contact with his skin. The coroner noticed petechiae on his neck and swabbed it. It turned up positive for the poison. The coroner is really puzzled because it's not something that a normal person would get into."

I tip-toed into the bathroom and eyed the tub. "Uncle Chris, how well do you know Ian and his brother?" I jerked the shower curtain back, heart pounding.

"Mm, I was wondering when you were going to ask me about him."

"You were?" I opened the linen closet.

"That brain of yours, always spinning just like your dad."

I resisted rolling my eyes. He needed some encouragement to

get into his storytelling mode. I gave him a little verbal nudge. "So you knew them when they were young?"

"Yeah," he said. I could hear him chewing. "We all started racing at the same time. I lived to beat them."

"What the heck are you eating?" I asked, giving my house the all clear. I walked back into the kitchen and started a pot of coffee.

"Pretzels," he crunched. I could practically imagine the crumbs spraying.

I continued. "Were his brother and Ian close back then?"

"They had a complicated relationship. His brother, Jordan, had a hot temper. He was even-keeled for the most part, but if you set him off, watch out. I remember one time when he stabbed a screwdriver through the driver's side window because the pit crew was too slow."

"Oh, my. Did Ian have that same temperament?"

"To be honest, I trusted Ian less. With Jordan, pretty much what you saw was what you got. But Ian was a salesman. He could sell you anything. Usually, stuff he didn't believe in himself."

"Really?"

"Yeah, and the thing he sold the most of was himself. He was everyone's friend. Or so they thought. No one suspected behind those wide eyes and big grin was someone who was ruthless."

"Did you ever see him be ruthless?"

"The way he came about buying his first race car was a little suspicious. He had a girlfriend, and she died. Weirdly enough, there was a life insurance policy on her and Ian was the benefactor. Cops never got him though."

"Wow. That's a little freaky." I thought of the thin man. He'd seemed nervous, with thin fingers plucking at his clothes and phone, and wine glass. Was he someone who had killed a person? Had that person's family gotten revenge? This suddenly seemed much more complicated. "Have you seen him do anything crazy recently? Is it possible that he made someone so angry that they decided to murder him?"

"Sure. I believe that in a heartbeat. But the only ones at that party were us. And I can't fathom that any of us did it."

"So, what do you think happened?"

His voice lowered. "To Ian? Honestly, this is one of the worst situations I've found myself in. A good friend killed, and only good friends there to witness it."

"Could it be someone who's not a friend? What about the neighbor?"

Uncle Chris hummed. "That guy seemed to be getting along with him when he showed up. Ian didn't seem upset to see him at all."

"Maybe someone was hired to do it. Like some weird delivery guy or someone we didn't see?"

"Maybe so, but that still means one of us did the hiring."

"Well, maybe not. What if it was one of the companies Ian used to work for. Or maybe someone at his new job didn't want him to transfer."

"I guess any one of those is a possibility. But how to go about proving it, that's the problem."

It was overwhelming to think about chasing down all these loose ends. I decided to change the subject. "You know, I'm still getting a hard time about having a Flamingo as our mascot. Especially in Pennsylvania."

Uncle Chris cleared his throat. "So, what do you say?"

"I say you lost a bet, of course. But I don't know if that makes our reality sound very reputable."

He snorted. "People will believe what they want to believe. As long as I'm selling, that's all I care about. Speaking of doing the opposite of what people expect, did you ever get a chance to check out that Challenger you wanted?" He laughed. "Your dad's going to have a fit."

"Nah, it was gone by the time I went back." It was a huge disappointment, to be honest.

He laughed even harder.

"What's so funny?" I demanded.

"It's just that the old saying is true. The apple don't fall far from the tree."

"What do you mean?" I asked.

"Didn't your old man ever tell you about his hot rod days?"

My eyes popped open What? My straight-laced, white-collar dad had hot rod days? "Tell me."

"Girl, who do you think got me into muscle cars? It was your father."

My father? The one who scolded me when I'd first brought up my dream as a teenager? The one who wore a tie even around the house?

"You're kidding me," I gasped.

"I'm totally serious. He had this sweet little 'Cuda that he later gifted to me. We used to take that thing over this sharp hill in town and jump over the railroad tracks."

"Seriously?"

"Yeah. We'd sneak out at night, all of us. Sadly, it ended the night the cops followed us home."

"Why would Dad go home if they were following you guys?"

"They were sneaky themselves and met us coming the other way. We got boxed in on our street." He laughed, and I heard a crunch of another pretzel. "Mom wasn't too happy with us."

"Your dad wasn't there?"

"Sweetie, Dad was never around."

That statement said a lot. But at the same time, back then, there were a lot of absentee parents. It didn't explain all the hostility he still had pent up towards Oscar.

We finished our conversation. I'd briefly thought about bringing up the black truck, but he hung up before I had the chance. I was also disappointed he didn't mention our previous planned meeting for Darcy's Doughnuts. I was starting to think that he'd forgotten that he'd even called me to talk about it. He *had* been pretty drunk that night.

Sighing, I locked my deadbolt and peeped out the window. Snow was falling again, covering up all signs that I'd been out jogging.

And covering up the tire tracks, as well.

13

I poured myself a mug of fresh steaming coffee and mused over these interesting details of my dad and Uncle Chris running from the police. It made me wonder if my mom was a part of that.

I gasped, realizing at that moment that I didn't know my mother's maiden name. I'd just known her as Vani O'Neil. Suddenly, that seemed like the most horrible thing ever, to not know her name. Could I find it on the internet? I opened up my browser, and my finger hovered over the search button.

My hand froze. The enormity of what I was about to do hit me. For the first time, ever, I was going to try to find information about my mom.

What if I found her?

My stomach nervously flopped like it was full of baby frogs. The feeling immediately grew worse, chest tightening, body screaming I needed to escape. I was actually having a panic attack. I couldn't do it. I was the biggest chicken in the world, but I couldn't look to see if she was alive.

Feeling small and gross at my cowardice, I set the phone on the counter. It rang just as it touched the surface, making me squeal in surprise. I stared at it for a second as crazy thoughts zoomed through my head. Was it my mother?

Good grief, woman, you don't even know if she's still alive. Of course, it's not. I snatched it up in both rage and bravado.

It was Kari.

"Hello?" I answered.

"Oh, good! You're there. I was afraid I'd have to leave a message, and you know how I hate to do that."

I did know. Most of Kari's messages were rambling nonsense that ended with, 'call me,' while conveniently leaving out any true intent for the reason she called in the first place.

"What's up?" I asked.

"I was just thinking about this weekend. What do you think you'll wear? I think you should go with that cute mini-skirt you had on last summer."

"I wore it because it was hot. Summer. Short skirts. They kind of go together, you know." I said dryly. "Unlike how they go with snowstorms and freezing temperatures."

"Freezing temperatures! Please, it's been a practically balmy winter for us. Maybe wear a pair of leggings with it. With those cute boots."

"I don't own any leggings without holes in them. Give it up, I'm wearing jeans."

"Listen, I know you're way out there in Timbuktu, so I don't think you remember what you should wear when you go out and socialize."

She was making me sound like a dog. "I am socialized," I answered, hotly. "And if you keep this up, I'll be wearing my overalls. Complete with cow crap."

She laughed. "I just want you to have fun."

"I'm doing this for you, remember. It's called being a sport. You actually owe me one."

"Well, it will be good for you, as well. You need to get out of the house. I half-expect to discover you're growing hair on your toes, what with your house in the hill and all."

I knew what she was doing. She knew what she was doing. And any single woman my age who has been set up more times than she could count knows that they never worked out. I was getting kind of sick playing her charade.

"I can do it on my own, thank you. I don't need a blind date."

"Date? Who said anything about a date? Just four people having a fun evening together. Come on. Don't be scared. Wear the skirt."

"I doubt it," I answered. "But I'll wear something nice."

"Oh, terrific! You're going to have such a fun time! Joe and I got his parents to watch the kids so it will be wine o'clock all night!"

I chuckled. "I'll see you then."

We hung up.

All right. So I know I need to get out more. And today kind of showed me maybe there was such a thing as being too isolated. I shivered at the thought of the black truck. I'd definitely keep my eye open for it around town. It had to be local. Who could it be?

THE NEXT DAY started the same way, with me fumbling for my coffee maker that hadn't turned on with the timer for the millionth time, and trying to find my phone.

The coffee maker obviously had problems but now was happily percolating. Phone was hidden under a pile of junk mail. As I picked it up, the screen warned me it only had twenty percent of the battery left. I groaned. Why did I keep forgetting to charge this thing?

I plugged it in and went back for coffee. It wasn't quite finished, but I needed a cup now. I grimaced at the strength and eased into my broken-down armchair (still amazingly comfortable) to check my emails.

Nothing. No new inquiries, no new clients. Even Jennifer and Mark hadn't sent me anything. I typed off a message asking if there was anything I could show them, and then stumbled for the shower.

I'd forgotten to take one the day before. Forgotten, or had been too lazy, take your pick. Anyway, I felt like I'd finished a huge achievement when I climbed out. TaDa world! I took a shower!

I dried my hair when my phone dinged. I ran over, hopeful that it was a new client but it was just Kari. **—can't wait to see you for dinner!**

I groaned like I was ready to heave up breakfast. How did I let myself get talked into stuff like this? I knew exactly what it was going to be like... awkward small talk with some strange man while Kari and Joe blinked cartoon heart-eyes at us with satisfied smiles.

Blech.

Still, she had brought up an important fact. Yesterday was a good start, but I needed to continue to shake loose the complacency that made me act like a home hobbit, like she inferred. But, since I really didn't want a repeat of what happened yesterday, I needed to find a new place to run.

Which meant only one thing.

I needed to join a gym. The introvert in me screamed, but I reasoned that it was the best of both worlds since I could wear headphones and zone out, but I was still around people.

Pulling up the search engine, I hunted for a highly rated local gym. Finally, I found one that seemed like it would work. The tag-line even said, "No pressure, no judgment. Work at your own pace."

That's exactly what I needed.

With no clients to help, I decided to head over there. There was no time like the present.

ABOUT TWENTY MINUTES LATER, I pulled into the parking lot for Pump gym—coincidentally located in the same lot as a teriyaki place and a cinnamon bun store; whose sweet scents nearly sabotaged my exercise plans. I persisted, marching past the bakery and up to the gym door, my chest swelling with pride that I was such a strong person.

I was met at the door by a very fit man. Very, very fit. Muscles bulged on top of muscles, all tan and shining, and he made sure they were on display in his tight tank top. He glanced at me, taking in my oversized sweats, baggy shirt, old shoes and ponytail, and probably marked me as a wannabe gym loser.

Well, he had that right. I definitely was no gym rat.

"Thanks," I said as he held the door open. I was surprised when he flashed me a friendly, slightly flirty grin.

"Hey there. New here?" he asked.

I was right that he marked me as a newbie. Still, the smile was amicable. I smiled back and nodded. "Yep. New in town. I need a place to run in this weather and thought I'd try it out here."

"Of course!" he said. "My name's Robbie. Come on over to the counter and I'll get you set up."

I followed him to the counter, a sterile piece of white Formica brilliantly lit by overhead fluorescents. Behind him were colorful displays of water bottles and fitness supplements.

"So, you must work here?" I asked as he pulled a keyboard up onto the counter from some place underneath the desk.

He grinned, perfect white teeth on a perfectly tanned face. "This is my place, actually. I've owned it for the last three years. I'll tell you what, it was a mess when I first got it but I've been working on it. Updating it. It's a nice place now. I think you'll like it. Your name?" he asked.

"Stella O'Neil."

He frowned for a second as he typed it in, using just his index fingers in a funny pecking motion. I braced myself for what I knew was coming, the infamous Flamingo accusation.

"You're the one with that flamingo?" he asked, jabbing a finger toward me.

"Yup," I nodded.

"Huh. That's funny." He grinned. "Tell me, what's a flamingo doing representing a realty company up here in Pennsylvania?"

"An old bet gone wrong."

"Not too wrong," he noted with a final tap to the keys. "It brought you out here." He smiled and turned the keyboard toward me. He also tipped the screen so I could read it. "If you could type how you found us and make sure I have your name right."

I eyed it and stifled a smile. He'd typed my name in hot pink.

"For the flamingo," he said, raising a thick eyebrow.

I typed in *internet* and passed the keyboard back. He read it, typed some more, and then put the keyboard away. Then he came out with a thin card which he stamped 10 times.

"Here, take this. This will give you a good long time to test out our gym. I think you're going to like it here."

I accepted the card and tucked it into my wallet. "Thank you."

He walked from behind the counter, showing a gracefulness that belied his size. Along with him came a scented spicy cloud. Maybe cinnamon. Not too strong and it smelled nice. "All right, follow me. I'll give you the grand tour."

We walked into the gym where the scent was stronger, along with an undercurrent of sweat.

"It's our disinfectant that you're smelling." He pointed to spray bottles that were scattered about with towels. "We have those available for everyone to spray down the equipment after they use it."

"Smells zesty," I noted.

"It's all natural, made from those essential oils. I'm not too big into chemicals. Still, don't spray it on your skin or anything. Your body can absorb it."

"What about my hands?" I said, lifting my palms.

"They're tough. They'll be fine. Just wash them when you're finished. You should do that anyway, with all the viruses nowadays."

My eyebrows flickered at his little biology education, but I nodded.

He showed me the classrooms where I could take any class, from dancing to spin, and then pointed out the men's and women's locker rooms, each with their own steam baths.

As we walked past the area for the weights—lined with mats and walls covered in mirrors, he asked me if I lifted.

I shook my head. "No. Running is my thing. I've done it since school."

"Well, we have the state-of-the-art treadmills right over here." He pointed toward them. Each had its own mini TV screen built in, among all the other options. "What did you run?"

"Mid-distance."

"Nice! In high school?"

I thought about my brief experience in college, and almost didn't bring it up, but then I decided I was going to be okay with the good, the bad, and the ugly. "I did one season in college, but I ended up losing every race." I shrugged. "I quickly found out I wasn't the star I'd thought I was in high school."

He smiled and nodded. "Same experience here."

"Really?" I said.

"Well, for me it was football. I really thought I was something else. College sure brought me down a peg or two."

Interesting. There definitely was more to him than I'd originally suspected.

He led me over to the treadmill and spent a little longer than he needed to in explaining to me how it worked. Finally, he left, and I started a warm up.

I brushed my hair behind my ears and caught a hint of spiciness. He wasn't joking that your skin picked up those essential oils.

I jogged for thirty minutes, not bad for my second time back in it. My ankles felt strong, and my muscles remembered why I loved this. When I finally turned the machine off, I was hot and sweaty and starving. Grabbing the spray bottle, I sprayed the machine and wiped it down, then headed to the locker room where I cleaned off as best as I could. A few minutes later, I headed out.

"I'll be seeing you!" Robbie called as I approached the door.

"Washed my hands," I joked, waving them at him.

He laughed, and I waved again before swinging my backpack up on my shoulder. My stomach growled, and I knew just where to go.

14

To be honest, I didn't go where my stomach was calling me. Between resisting that cinnamon bun place and Darcy's Doughnuts, with their sweet jelly-filled confectionary delights, I was feeling like the queen of self-control. Instead, I chose the Springfield Diner. Ostentatiously, I told myself I would be good and order a salad. However, the scent of freshly cut French fries changed my mind faster than a Vegas dealer shuffling cards. I mean, there was only so much self-control a person could have.

The waitress waltzed over to seat me, but not before Marla Springfield spotted me from the kitchen. She was the founder of this restaurant, and we'd become friends over the last few months.

"Stella!" Marla walked up, and I smiled. She wore her

characteristic chintz apron and tiny glasses. "How are you, love?" The woman was old, in her eighties, and thin as a matchstick. I swear I could see the nobs of her spine through the back of her dress. But she had that wiriness and determination in her steps that warned you not to underestimate her.

"Well now, Miss Stella. What are you hungry for today?" Her eyes twinkled behind her glasses.

"I'm starving," I admitted.

"You here for my five-alarm chili?" She led me over to a table and pointed for me to sit.

"What's that?" I asked, slightly concerned.

"Little anchos, smoked meat, no beans." She leaned over to straighten the napkin.

I'd never heard of anchos. "What's the first thing you said?"

"Anchos. They're little peppers."

"Aw, we should get them a hat."

She looked confused.

"You know, because they're little chilly." Proof my blood sugar was low. I was cracking corny jokes.

Her lips puckered, crinkling with wrinkles at the edges, like the rays of the sun. I thought I'd either lost her or offended her. I was gearing for trouble when she busted out a cackle. Patrons at the table next to me smiled at the sound, and I grinned, too. Who wouldn't? Here was this cute eighty-year-old woman practically busting a gut.

"Get them hats! I've got to tell that one to Ralph!" She squinted at me. "Now what are you doing here all sweaty-like? You still working at the realty office? You don't go to work looking like that, do you?"

I plucked at my t-shirt to fan myself out and then winced, imagining the wave of sweat I probably just gave her. "Just got back from the gym."

"Huh. Gym, hmm? You know, I don't abide in all that fancy paying-to-sweat-in-a-building stuff. Good hard work will keep you in shape." She flexed her arm, and the muscle jumped like a rubber band. "Keeps me strong."

"You definitely are," I admired.

"Now, what have you been selling lately?" She leaned a bony hip against the table and watched me expectantly.

"Right now, I just have one client. They were going to buy the Stuber's place until—" I left it there, figuring she was so on top of the gossip that she'd understand.

Her near non-existent eyebrows puckered their few white

hairs together. "Ahh, I see. So you're trying to find them a new place?"

I nodded.

"Well good. They may have squeaked out of a bad deal and need to be thankful."

"I'm not sure about that. They loved that place."

Her mouth pursed and she stared me straight in the eye. "There's such a thing as a house of love, and then there's a strange home. Those two couldn't be more different. That place there is a strange home. And the neighbors made sure to do their part to keep it that way."

There was something alarming in the way she said that. "I know they didn't get along, but they seemed to have patched it up at the end. Or is there something I'm missing?"

She leaned down so her joints cracked in her back. I winced at the sound.

"Those two were sitting just over there. A couple of weeks ago." She pointed to a table about three over from mine. "Talking ugly talk. Gordon told Ian that he could send the gardener back in a box if he gave them any more trouble. Gave me the shivers to hear."

"Wow, they seemed so nice at the party." I held back that Oscar had mentioned that Gordon had mob ties.

"Not everything is as it seems, young lady. And it's high time you learned that. Now, how about that chili? It's won more contests than you can shake a stick at."

"Mm, I'm thinking a chicken wrap this time," I said with an apologetic shrug. Chili and I weren't the best of friends, and I only had one roll of toilet paper left at home.

Her joints crackled again as she leaned away from the table. "You know, I saw the Valentines the other day."

"Really?" Those two octogenarian siblings had been on my mind for a while ever since I saw Charity at the nursing home. It was interesting that Marla was bringing them up, considering there'd been a long-standing grudge between both her and the Valentines for going on sixty years now. "Did you actually talk with them?"

Her eyes softened as she smiled. "They say that time heals all wounds. I'd say that in the case of our squabble, it sure did."

"She apologized?" I gasped, a little dubious.

"Pshaw. At our age, you don't apologize for nothing. No. She asked for a slice of my pumpkin pie, and then she said it was right good. Course, then she tacked on that she seemed to remember giving me the recipe, of which I had to give a sharp rebuttal."

"And?" I asked, trying to picture this argument.

"And, we're right as rain. She's changed a lot through the years. They come to have their Sunday night pot roast here along with the rest of the folks."

"Aw, that makes me happy. I saw Charity volunteering the other day. It's nice to see they're doing well."

The bell rang from the back. She sent a scowl in that direction that would've made a truck driver shiver. "I'm coming, I'm coming!" And then back to me, "The Valentines are tough. They're survivors. And they've learned to survive by keeping their nose out of other people's business. You know, Miss Stella, you could learn that trick yourself. A young woman like yourself needs to be careful."

I swallowed hard, thinking about the black truck. "What do you mean?"

"I mean, Ian Stuber had some enemies." She leaned in close and I swear her ancient body creaked again. "Some bad people who are hearing tell of you asking questions."

"Bad people? How do you know this?"

"I may be old, but I've always been a listener." She tapped her ear. "And these things haven't failed me yet."

He ears were large and stuck out prominently from under her hair that was held with several bobby pins on top of her head.

The lobes dangled, wrinkled. Still, there were no hearing aids.

"What have you heard?" I asked. "And who's talking?"

"I'm hearing rumors is all. Little airy rumors." She waggled wrinkled fingers. "About some pretty young brunette who is poking her nose where it doesn't belong. I'm telling you right now, you leave that stuff to the police."

"How come these rumors aren't going after the police?" I asked. "They ask harder questions than I ever have."

"The police know how to do their dealings in this town. And it's not by ruffling feathers. You want to make sure you don't ruffle any yourself. You're just one lonely chick in this great big world, and you're catching the eyes of a few too many chicken hawks."

The bell dinged again, and this time the cook yelled, "Order up!

She sighed and straightened her apron ties. "Now, I'll go put your order in for that chicken wrap. And, while I'm at it, can I get you a piece of my homemade apple crisp?"

"Sorry, just the chicken wrap today," I said, a little stunned and mortified that people had been talking about me. What had I said to get them starting? And who was it? The guy in the black truck?

I took a sip of water, trying to sort through what she said. I'd seen cops in here eating breakfast before. Was Marla trying to warn me that the cops were dirty?

Prickles rose on my neck like I was being watched. My gaze darted around the restaurant, but everyone seemed to be focused on their food and table guests. Seconds ticked by. I waited for the feeling to pass, but it didn't.

Someone was staring. I could feel it.

The waitress named Tammy, came over with my lunch and sat it down. I grinned to see a small cup of chili sitting next to my wrap. I raised up my hand to order a drink, but she blazed away like there was a million-dollar tip on some table in the back. For some unknown reason, she'd never liked me, and always gave me a hard time whenever she had to serve me.

That must be it, I convinced myself. I must have subconsciously seen she was here and felt that animosity. That's why I thought someone was watching me. Feeling better, I picked up my chicken wrap and was gearing to take a bite, when my eyes locked onto a man sitting a few tables away. He stared brazenly back. I hurriedly glanced away, only to see a woman watching me from two tables over. My cheeks flushed, and I glanced down at my french fries.

You're just freaking out, after what Marla said. After a

moment, I peeked at the two of them again, and both were seemingly absorbed with their conversations.

After I finished, I waved down my waitress. Tammy came over, her hand in her greasy apron pocket.

"I was just wondering if I could get my check."

"Oh, I meant to tell you. It's been paid for." She looked down her nose like I didn't deserve it.

"Really?" I smiled, thinking Marla must have treated me.

"Yeah. Some man. He said he'd been watching you real close, and he wanted to remind you that you're never alone."

Her words hit me like I'd just opened the door of an arctic freezer. "What are you talking about?" Some man? Watching me? "What did he look like?"

She gathered my dishes. "I'm too busy to pay attention to stuff like that. Left me a twenty and said to tell you what I just said." She leaned back with her hands full and an impatient look on her face. "Now will there be anything else?"

My mind was spinning. "Have you seen him before?"

She shrugged. "You work in this town long enough, you've seen everyone. Now, if you don't mind, I need to get to my other tables. I don't have time to be yakking."

I rubbed my forehead, wondering if I should call the police. Just then, goosebumps prickled my arms. Someone was watching me again. Right now. I could feel it. Staring at me from somewhere behind. Slowly, I turned around. There, at the window, a figure darted away.

I ran to the restaurant's door, bumping into chairs on the way, and yanked open the door. No one was there. All I could think about was the guy in the black truck. Would he be following me home tonight?

15

The rest of the day was spent on me being a chicken. Chicken, chicken. I didn't want to even check my emails. I couldn't even read Grandma Wiktoria's letters because I didn't want to learn anything new. I wanted to curl up, take a bath, hide out and read. I needed to go some place different than I was, and a nice fiction book was going to take me there.

I didn't completely hide away. There was an email from Jennifer and Mark with a request for a house showing for the next day. I scheduled it and responded back to them with the confirmation.

Then I did do some self-protecting. I'm going to term it "self-care," because I like that better. And it was true. I needed some down time where I felt safe. Book, candle, lavender bubble bath. I went to bed that night feeling much better.

The next morning, I met the Clarks outside the gate of a cute community. I punched in the code and we drove through the entrance.

The houses in this neighborhood were all newer. I knew the agent representing this place, Angela Cranton, and I suspected she'd be there today. She wasn't my favorite person, what with her snooty attitude she had since she normally represented the more elite clients. Still, we all needed to get along as best as we could in this business, sort of a 'you scratch my back, I'll scratch yours' scenario. However, there was an unwritten rule that all of us agents understood as well —if you touch my client list, prepare for those scratches to turn into stabs.

We pulled into the driveway, a lovely flagstone that was flanked by myrtle bushes. There was a little turn-around where we parked. It was a beautiful sunny day, and the sky unseasonably clear for winter.

I walked over to them, rubbing my hands together. The sun had tricked me and I was poorly dressed in a short-sleeve shirt. "So, did you ever get a chance to share the conversation you heard with the police?"

Jennifer nodded. "It was actually an interesting interview. I'd forgotten one part that we'd overheard. I think they were fighting over landscaping as well."

"What? Like hedges and flowers and stuff?" I asked. Was that code word for something?

"Yeah, Ian screamed that he was going to more than fire the landscaping guy."

Just then, the front door of the house opened and Angela Cranton, in all her hairspray, clown make-up and tight-business-suit glory, toddled out in high heels.

"Oh, my word! Fancy meeting you here, Stella!" she shrieked from the porch. Of course, Angela knew I'd be here. She knew everything about my clients by now. She toddled down the stairs and linked arms with Jennifer. "How is your agent treating you? Stella's new in the business, so you have to give her a chance. But here, let me give you my card—"

"Angela!" I snapped.

At my voice, Angela backed off with her hands up in mock surrender. "Sorry, sorry. I just want to help. I know how it is when you work in a tiny realty office such as your own. Now come in! Let me show you this hidden gem!"

WE SPENT A HEADACHE-INDUCING HOUR THERE, with Angela fawning over both the Clarks and the house. She knew her stuff though, and it seemed like both Jennifer and Mark were eating up what she was serving. We left with the couple saying they wanted to talk it over privately, but I fully expected them to contact me to make an offer before the day was through.

I parked in front of the Flamingo agency and walked in. Kari on her way out.

"So, we still on for this weekend?" she asked. Her grin was entirely too cheery and starting to make me feel stabby. Honestly, she was starting to be obnoxious with the amount of times she was bringing the dinner up. I nodded, barely.

"Good!" Her adamant nod slowed, and she eyed me with consideration. "You know, I have someone else you have to meet."

I groaned. "Please, Kari...."

"No, not a date. My good friend, Georgie. The three of us need to get together someday. She's just started dating a guy, so she completely understands what it means to have those lean years."

"Lean years?" I asked with an arched eyebrow, daring her to elaborate.

She caught the look right away and hurried to rephrase it. "You know, lean for companionship. Not that it's wrong..." She bit her lip and then blurted. "I can't keep this charade up. You know what happens if you never get out? You never shave your legs or anything else, and the hair becomes junglefied. And then you start collecting cats and eating out of Chinese take-out boxes."

"What's wrong with that?" I raised my arm, and pulled open my shirt sleeve, flashing her my pit.

"See what I mean!" she shrieked.

I laughed. "I've had boyfriends. This is the winter coat." Actually, I generally liked to keep things smooth. I just happened to need a new razor and was sick of getting nicked. It was a good opportunity to yank her chain.

"Oh, my gosh!" she huffed and stormed out.

I was still grinning as I strolled to my desk. I filed my paperwork and then checked my email for messages.

"Anything?" Uncle Chris asked, sauntering out of his office. He was looking pretty sharp in a blue suit and purple tie.

I shook my head. "I'm thinking they're going to want to put in an offer though. They really liked the house."

"All right, sounds good. Let's get them buttoned up and

under contract." He stuck his hands into his pocket. "You eat yet? I'm about to go grab some lunch. Want to come with?"

My jaw dropped at his suggestion. Was this it? Was this the moment where he finally was going to tell me the news that he'd hinted at during the drunken phone call?

16

I wasn't sure what Uncle Chris was going to say, and my expression must have shown it.

"Why's your mouth open like that?" he asked, scowling. "Don't look so shocked. I'm not that much of a cheapskate."

"No, you just took me by surprise," I said, scrambling for my purse and my jacket. I shrugged into it as I followed him out to the parking lot. "Where we going?"

"Just back here. One of my favorite places."

He led me around the building to a taco vendor parked in the empty lot behind the realty.

"Wow! When did this show up?" I asked. There were a few people in line ahead of us. The delicious scent of melted cheese and fresh salsa promised a tantalizing meal.

"Isn't this great? They always come around this time of year. You want a taco? Their taquitos are the best."

"Yeah, sure," I nodded. I wondered how they'd compare to the ones I'd grown up with around Seattle. We had some of the best back in Washington.

Finally, it was our turn. Uncle Chris ordered and gave her a twenty. A minute later, the woman handed over paper plates wrapped in tin-foil.

"Come on, let's sit over here." He headed over to about a half dozen picnic benches, zeroing in on one like it was his spot. I figured that proved he'd been here a time or two.

A gusty sigh eased out of him as he sat down. I sat across from him. Carefully, I picked off the foil and took a bite.

Delicious.

"Good food, right?" he grunted.

I nodded. "So, how are you doing?"

"I'm confused," he confessed. "I've been going over in my mind who I think could have done it. The cops seem to be hinting that it must have been his wife."

I thought about the blonde, petite woman. "Why Jasmine?"

"Well, she kind of married him in a weird way."

"Really? How's that?" I took another bite and hummed in satisfaction.

"He met her at the Cowboy Bar and Grill. She had this big sob story. Something about her rent being due, and the manager of the restaurant hitting on her. She was crying to Ian because that dirt bag wouldn't leave her alone."

That actually really did sound like a terrible situation. "Okay."

"Ever since I've known him, Ian always fell for that damsel in distress act."

I picked at a piece of lettuce. "So she's probably the sole inheritor, right?"

"Seems that way."

I chewed and thought some more. It really didn't make sense to me. She had what she wanted, at least on the outside. A lovely life, clothing, jewelry. Friends and traveling.

Not to mention the few times that I'd spoken with her, she'd come across so meek. It was hard to imagine her swatting a fly, let alone cold-bloodedly poisoning her husband and leaving him to die in the bathroom.

Still, I wasn't the best judge of people.

"What about the neighbors?" I asked.

"Neighbors?"

"Yea, that Gordon guy just showed up, and they brought that wine. From what I'm hearing, they couldn't stand each other. You remember how you were worried they were going to cause trouble when we put the sign up? Plus, I've heard that Gordon has mob ties."

"What? Who are you hearing this from?"

I blushed. I really didn't want to say Oscar. "Mmm, maybe Jan from the post office. You know how gossip is."

"Jan from the Post Office?" His eyebrows lifted.

I nodded.

"Are you referring to that lady who talks to her cat all day? That's your great source of information?"

I'd forgotten about her orange tabby, Skittles, that lived behind the counter. I bit a hangnail and nodded. "She watches out the window and really knows stuff. And..." I didn't want to say any more. The incredulous look on his face had dropped into an expression of hilarity. He rubbed his mouth with his hand, struggling to contain it. I was afraid just one more word would push him into a burst of laughter at me.

"Never mind," I said, focusing on my food.

He shook his head. "As far as I know, Ian Stuber and Gordon Taylor were friends at the end. Sure, there was some trouble over garbage cans and dogs barking, but they were both mature enough to let by-gones be by-gones."

"What if that was an act? Like maybe Gordon poisoned him to get revenge. Both he and his wife did show up at the party uninvited and gave Ian wine that only he drank."

"How on earth would they know that he would drink it?" He frowned. "Besides, from what the coroner said, it was topical."

Topical, huh? I chewed thoughtfully and swallowed. "Maybe the neighbor jabbed him with a needle."

"Stella, don't you think Ian would have said something if that happened? At least yelped? Not to mention, what would the Taylor's have to gain by such a risky action? The guy was moving."

I rubbed my temple. "I don't know. It makes little sense." After a second, I tacked on, "What about Ian's brother? What was his name? You said he had a hot temper."

"Jordan. And that feels like even more of a stretch. That was his brother, after all. And he wasn't at the party."

I nodded. "I guess so. But somebody must have done it."

We both continued eating until it became apparent that

Uncle Chris was allowing the silence to grow. He shifted uncomfortably. I watched him out of the corner of my eye, sensing it was time to give him space.

"Hey, Stella." A serious expression settled into the lines around his mouth.

I held my breath. This was it. The moment he was about to spill his guts. I could feel it. I tensed in preparation.

"I—ugh—I have a favor to ask."

A favor? I was caught off guard with the possibilities. "What is it?"

"I was wondering if you'd accompany me to Ian's memorial service. It's this weekend." His countenance was conflicted.

"Oh." Many thoughts raced through my mind, with HECK NO leading the pack. I barely knew how to comfort people as it was, let alone leave me in a room full of grieving strangers. And, for some reason, my discomfort wasn't obvious, and I always became the magnet that people wanted to hug. I never knew what to say and ended up sounding like an idiot by mumbling, "There, there," while uncomfortably patting their shoulder. Despite my best efforts, I think I was more like the anti-comforter. Uncle Chris wanted me to come?

Still, it wasn't often he'd ask me for something. I mean, yeah, he did ask me to grab him a coffee a few times, and he'd asked me to put the sign up the other day. There was that one time he asked me to get his dry cleaning.

But not really *ask* me something. Something that caused his eyes to crinkle in pain while he frowned.

I nearly gasped at my next thought. Uncle Chris was relying on me like family. This was probably new for him as well, what with being estranged from Oscar and not having the greatest relationship with my dad. I bet the nearest thing he'd had as family all this time were his old racing buddies.

Suddenly, I felt honored. I felt like a pillar he was leaning on, and I was determined to be strong for him.

"Absolutely," I said with an emphatic nod.

"You will?" His face relaxed, even as his voice sounded surprised.

"Of course."

"It's just that with his brother there and his mom...his wife. I feel overwhelmed." His face fell into a frown again. "Even worse, they asked me to speak at the memorial."

"Aw, you're going to be great!" I said. "Who better to say who he was than one of his best friends."

"You think so?"

I was taken back by this glimpse of his insecurity. He always appeared so confident to the point of blustery.

"Yes, I absolutely do. Besides, this will give me a good opportunity to watch for any weird behavior."

He groaned. "I can just see it now. Don't be giving everyone the evil eye."

"I would never!"

He snorted. "Are you kidding me? Your face shows everything. I can even tell when your coffee's cold."

"I'll wear my most impervious mask of non-emotion," I declared. "What time do we need to be there?"

"Starts at one." He'd taken a big bite and talked around it. "Afterwards is like a reception or something."

Just talking about the funeral set my teeth on edge. That was going to be a surreal day, seeing all the very same people that had been at his party just a few days before.

"See, I can tell right now you're dreading it. It's written all over your face."

"Don't worry, I've got this. My thoughts will strictly be thinking of ways to support you."

"Thank you," he said. "I appreciate that. But do me a favor, and just be a normal guest. Don't look at anyone like they're mobsters. Keep your private eye hat off that day."

I nodded. I would definitely keep my face neutral.

But deep down, he had to know that I'd definitely be watching for anything out of the ordinary.

*A*fter lunch, I remembered I needed to renew my license. Because I was in a new state, I had to go visit the DOL, rather than doing it online as I could in Washington.

I didn't even know where the DOL was. Uncle Chris gave me the directions with a pitying look, and then we headed our separate ways. I actually had no trouble finding the building, but finding parking was another story. Two blocks later, I finally walked inside.

I grabbed my paper number and bit back a groan. The place was packed. I found a spot in the back, sat down and got out my phone, intending on being here for a while.

I'd only played one game of Tetris when I heard the front

door open and a high giggle. I glanced up and nearly jumped out of my skin when I saw that it was the Valentines. Every part of me shriveled with the word, "Nooooo." It wasn't Charity that was the problem—she was a doll. It was her sister, Gladys, whom I only referred to, even in my thoughts, as Ms. Valentine.

Charity had been quite charming when I'd run into her at the nursing home, but I didn't expect the same welcome from Ms. Valentine. She'd been furious with me the last time I'd seen her. In fact, the thought of that made me want to puke. Quickly, I looked for someplace to hide.

Unfortunately, the DOL doesn't offer many places. I considered leaving and coming back another day, but then the number clicked on the overhead boards, showing I was next in line. Blast it! I couldn't leave now. I raised the collar of my coat and ducked my head.

"But, Sister—"

"I have no choice, Charity. And quit your complaining. You sound like a teakettle gone scalding on the stove. It's of no use, that law's changed, and we have to do one final renew of our registration for the T-bird."

I shuddered at the mention of the car, a beast with round headlights that had chased me one night. It was so similar to what had happened the other day, but the T-bird had been driven by their brother who was in jail now. That makes two people who've chased me in motor vehicles. What was it with me and cars?

They walked to the front in a wafting cloud of wool coats and violet perfume. Ms. Valentine snatched a paper from the counter and stared hard at the screen above the desks.

"All right, we have a number. Fifty-one. Wonderful. Looks like we'll be here all day," she harrumphed. "Let's go find a seat."

I crouched lower in my jacket and stared hard at my phone, mentally cursing my choice to come today.

Clicking heels came closer. I was practically pop-eyed at the concentration I was giving my phone.

Pointed brown shoes stopped squarely in front of me.

"Well, well, well. If it isn't our lovely real estate agent, Ms. O'Neil," Ms. Valentine said.

Nervously, I glanced up. Ms. Valentine stared down at me in her charming way, like I was a dirty tissue caught on the edge of her shoe.

"Oh! Ms. Valentine! Charity! How are the both of you?" I babbled, acting surprised.

"We are doing great, thank you." Charity smiled.

"Well, that's lovely." I glanced desperately at the counter, but it seemed the people before me were just beginning their transaction. "Have you settled into a new home, yet?"

"No. Every evening, we traipse from park bench to park bench since we sold the million dollar estate." Ms. Valentine rolled her eyes.

"Sister," Charity chided. My brows raised. I was surprised to hear that. She'd always been so subservient before.

"Of course, we have a new place," Ms. Valentine finally answered.

"It's really quite lovely," Charity prattled, butting in. I was relieved and gave her my full attention.

"Really! I'm so happy for you. It was fun seeing you at the nursing home the other day."

"That was quite timely, now wasn't it?" Charity said while Ms. Valentine turned narrowed eyes in her sister's direction. I guess Charity hadn't shared that. The short woman continued. "And how are you doing? We've seen those Flamingo for sale signs popping up all over Novelty Hill."

"Oh, Do you live close to that development?"

"We do! We have the cutest little home right on the corner. A lovely space. It has its own tea garden." Charity giggled.

My eyes raised. That was the same community Ian had lived in. "That sounds fun," I mumbled, the gears in my head turning.

"Of course, we know about poor Ian. We saw the flamingo come down yesterday. I don't suppose you're selling that place any more?" Charity pursed her eyebrows sympathetically.

"No, Jasmine has decided to stay at the house. Did you ever get a chance to meet them?" I asked.

"Just once. The wife came over with a pie." Charity sank into the chair next to me with a happy sigh.

"That wasn't his wife," Ms. Valentine sniffed.

"Oh? Who was it then?" I asked.

"That was their housekeeper."

"We haven't seen them since. The next day, their neighbor's, the Taylors came over. They had terrible things to say about the Stubers. It was shocking. I was scared to eat the pie after that, and you know how I love them." Charity raised her eyebrow.

"We wouldn't dream of socializing with either family. They both are uncouth," Ms. Valentine said. She eyed the plastic chairs, and her eyelids fluttered. "Charity, get up. That isn't sanitary."

"I'm tired, Sister. Just let me rest a moment." Charity pouted. Again, I was surprised to see her show a backbone. I guess it was true that it's never too late to change.

Ms. Valentine seemed to have accepted this new resolution in Charity because there wasn't the usual bullying response that I'd been accustomed to. Instead, she focused her pale blue eyes at the window, her lips primly set into disapproving lines.

But silent. I liked that.

"So, did you like the Taylors?" I asked Charity. "I don't remember his wife's name, but his name is Gordon."

"I can't remember her name either, but she was nice. Brought over a dozen roses from their garden. They smelled divine. I think they were those rare Ben Franklin ones. You know, the ones with the double petals?"

I didn't know, and with my green thumb more the shade of brown, it was unlikely I ever would. I nodded though, to encourage her deeper into conversation.

"They were so lovely. Do you think they'd let us have a clipping?" she asked her sister.

Ms. Valentine rolled her eyes, obviously displeased at her sister still not acknowledging the neighbor's uncouthness, or the lack of chair hygiene.

"Anyway, all she seemed to want to talk about was the Stubers. Apparently, there'd been an issue when Mr. Stuber built their fence. Or maybe they knocked over the fence. It was so hard to keep track of. And Mr. Stuber is rarely home, but when he is, he liked to race down the street in that fancy car of his. Plus there's quite a scandalous rumor that Mrs. Stuber is in love with her neighbor. However, Jeffry says quite the opposite."

"Charity Valentine! You are hardly any better than them with your gossiping tongue!"

"Oh, pooh! Who else is there to tell? Besides, we ran right into Stella here. That seems quite serendipitous!"

"Who's Jeffry?" I asked, trying to bring the conversation back to the target. I swear, this was about as easy as herding a litter of puppies.

"Jeffry is our gardener. He comes every Sunday. He also takes care of the Stuber's place. He's there quite a bit."

"And the Taylors's," Ms. Valentine piped in. She arched an eyebrow and glanced away as if not wanting to be caught acting interested.

"Really! What else did he say?" I asked.

"He says that Mr. Stuber was a complete boar. That he treated his poor wife something awful. I think he rather felt sorry for her." Charity paused, and a dreamy expression relaxed the lines around her eyes. "Jeffry is such a nice man. I half wonder if he fancies me."

Ms. Valentine snorted. "The man is simply reacting to you following and pestering him all the time. Don't get your hopes up. I swear, you're driving him to headaches. I saw him take some medicine the other day, just as he spotted you walking up. If he's gone then where will we be? I'd like to see you digging up the weeds."

"Sister, you are so unkind. Of course, no one knows how long they have. I myself take medicine." Her hand fluttered over her heart. "It's a terrible thing getting old."

Ms. Valentine snorted. "I didn't say he'd die, I said he'd leave. And as far as getting old, it's better than the alternative." She leaned on her cane, easing her weight to her other foot. I could only guess that she was regretting her stand against the 'filthy chairs'.

"Well, I still think he might fancy me. He does have such a smile when I come around."

"More likely a grimace," Ms. Valentine tacked on. "It's probably that infernal pesticide he's always mucking around the garden."

"He knows what he's doing. Did you know that Jeffry is a smuggler?" Charity's eyes widened like a school girl's. "Yes!

He was on a trip in China and discovered a mushroom that works miracles on powdery mildew. It's all natural, but quite toxic to touch while it's wet."

"Yikes! And you're sure it's safe?" I asked.

She nodded. "Once it's dry, it's perfectly fine. I've given a few rose clippings to several friends. No one's died yet!"

She giggled, but her wording sent chills down my spine. I didn't have time to respond though. At that moment, a ding announced the number had changed. I was finally up. I said my goodbyes and walked to the counter.

Those ladies were something else. I shook my head and gave my 'please, let everything go smoothly' smile to the attendant as I slid over my license and debit card. As she told me the price, I winced.

I really needed to get a house sold.

18

Saturday morning was cold and raining when Uncle Chris and I arrived at the church. Everything about funerals made my skin crawl. Not only did I hate watching people cry (and feel helpless to comfort them,) but I knew that someone in there, crowding shoulder to wool-jacketed shoulder—had to be guilty. I firmly ascribed to the theory that the murderer always showed up again. Maybe I'd learned it from TV shows, but it made sense to me. He or she needed that recognition even though they couldn't take credit for the crime. They craved to hear the drama and emotions, as well as the gossip.

But I kept my bargain to keep my face free from emotion. Uncle Chris took one look at me and whispered that I needed to quit sucking on that lemon. That was good for a laugh, which helped.

We found a seat on one of the hard pews, the floor damp around us from all the folded umbrellas. The service was long. I feel terrible for saying that, but it was. The priest spoke on and on about stuff that didn't seem to have anything to do with a funeral and sounded more like a recycled Sunday sermon. His message was interrupted at intervals by a tired-looking woman at the organ who thumped the pedals until the organ itself sounded like it was giving up the ghost.

People yawned around me. I blinked hard myself. Was there anyone here who cared about Ian?

A sniff to the right of me caught my attention. Uncle Chris. He pulled out a handkerchief and wiped his eyes. It yanked on my heartstrings and made me feel like an absolute heel.

At the end of the funeral, the priest invited us to the reception hall downstairs. He offered for the family to go first, and Jasmine, and another man whom I assumed was Ian's brother, along with an older couple filed past.

They stood in line just inside the entrance to the reception hall. We congregated outside and slowly rifled through the doors after expressing our condolences. Jasmine was calm but thin and pale, clad in a simple black dress. Her hand was ice cold when she took mine. Uncle Chris broke down again while shaking the brother, Jordan's, hand. I patted my uncle's back as we passed into the room.

There was already a line in place for people getting food.

Uncle Chris wiped his eyes. "You coming?" he asked.

I shook my head. "Maybe in a minute."

He nodded and, after straightening his sport's jacket, lumbered over, appearing like he was feeling slightly better. A group of men saw him coming and welcomed him with smiles and claps on the back.

I scanned along the line of people waiting in the reception line, searching for anyone acting suspicious or out of place. Everyone seemed focused on the buffet—mounds of chicken, platters of salad, a plethora of crock-pots.

Wait. Who was that lady?

A woman waited to the side, not quite in the line, but still by the tables. Her hands were tucked deep into the pockets of her tan dress coat, and she watched the crowd with a quiet stillness. That was quite curious to me. Who stood by themselves and stared like that?

A nano-second later, I realized I was acting exactly the same way. I blushed, realizing how I must stand out like a sore thumb here in the center of the room.

I started to move back to a place where it was less inconspicuous when I felt a touch on my shoulder. It was Kari.

"How are you doing, chickie?" she asked. She wore a somber dark blue sweater, her blonde hair pulled into a tight chignon.

I shrugged. "Better than Uncle Chris."

Kari raised her chin. "What do you think she's thinking about?"

I glanced in the direction she pointed.

Celeste.

She wore a silk, cream-colored dress and was posed like an ice queen. I'm serious, if a director were casting the part of a frigid ice-carving brought to life, she would get it, hands down. Blonde-white hair like corn silk, blue eyes as pale as a glacier's heart, skin that appeared already touched by frost.

"She's thinking she wants to get out of here, like the rest of us. I just saw her the other day at Jasmine's house," I said. "I had those papers that needed to be signed, remember? Well, I also brought over a piece of jewelry that I found when we were cleaning up after the party. They had no idea who it belonged to."

"Hm, must have belonged to some other guest."

I watched one of the young men from the reception line stare over at Celeste. He nodded at her as the corner of his mouth lifted, giving her a sultry expression like he thought he was trapping her under his spell. Slightly pouty lips, lowered eyebrows.

She gave him a cruel smile and turned away. Burn!

She must have felt my eyes on her because she glanced my way. Her eyebrows lifted in recognition and she sauntered over.

Next to me, Kari muttered, "Wonderful."

"Hello, ladies," Celeste said, lifting a wine glass. I wondered where she'd gotten it from.

"Celeste," nodded Kari.

I smiled back. "It's nice to see you again. I was just talking to Kari about the jewelry piece I found, and we were wondering who it could have belonged to."

"Who on earth knows," she said in a bored drawl.

I was a little taken aback by her response, unsure of what to say next. Luckily, Kari came to my rescue.

"Are you looking for someone, Celeste?" she asked.

"Mmm, trying to sense if Ruth's here. You know, Ian's mom." She took another sip and leisurely looked around. I shivered, not wanting to follow her gaze.

"Oh, really? And why do you think that's a possibility?" Kari asked, smiling, but I knew her well enough that the question was loaded with skepticism.

Her brow puckered. "Her boy was murdered. She might be here for justice."

Before Kari or I could respond, there was a noise from the front of the room in the form of nervous clearing of the throat into a microphone. Uncle Chris stood there, easing back and forth on his feet, getting ready to speak.

"If I could just have your attention," he said, his face red and sweaty. The microphone took a horrible turn for the worse as it emitted a high pitch squeal.

He cringed, and we all winced. I watched him pat his jacket front where he kept his cigar. Feeling it seemed to bolster him, and he continued.

"We all know how important family is. Well, Ian Stuber was family to me." The room quieted as Uncle Chris proceeded to share some of his memories of Ian. When he finished, the microphone was passed to a few more people.

There were tears and laughter. I relaxed, feeling like people here did care about Ian.

After the last person finished, Celeste lightly touched my elbow. "I need to go find Jasmine. She's probably a wreck."

I understood what she meant. Hearing all the speeches hit me in the heart too. I watched her slowly drift through the crowds in search for her cousin.

Unfortunately, Celeste had headed in the wrong direction. Here came Jasmine from the back where all the flowers were being displayed.

Walking in her direction to intercept her was an attractive man. Her drawn face lit up with a small smile as he clasped her hands in his. He started talking animatedly. They were too far away for me to eavesdrop, but his face was set in a firm, comforting expression and his words seemed to relax her.

Jasmine nodded as he spoke, and then answered him back. He seemed shocked at what she said, eyebrows raised, jaw open. Now, this was interesting. He nervously glanced across the room, and his hand left hers and went to the knot in his tie. He shrugged his shoulders as if his jacket were too tight, and then settled back into his confident persona as he answered her.

I waited for her response, but instead of giving one, she frowned and abruptly walked away.

Whoa. What was that all about? My gaze followed her for a second to see where she'd go. She was immediately detained by an older couple, both wearing matching cardigans and deeply sympathetic expressions.

I turned my attention back to the man. For a second, I couldn't find him. He had walked rather abruptly across the room. I finally spotted him near the refreshment table. He was staring at something in his hand. A piece of paper? His complexion flushed a deep red, and he angrily crumpled it up.

What in the world? His hand shook that was clutching the paper. He stormed over to the trash can and flung it in. After straightening his tie, he helped himself to a glass of juice, gulped it down, and threw the cup into the trash can with the same ferociousness.

Every nerve in me was on *go*, jerking me forward. I had to see what was on that paper. But before I could reach the trash can, a woman wearing a white straw hat, matching sweater, and a dark chintz dress threw a mucky pile of paper plates in the trash.

No!

She started to undo the bag to take it out.

I ran over, bumping people out of my way. "Excuse me. Sorry!" I muttered, in a panic.

I reached the trash can just as she was lifting it.

"Here! I'll take that!" I said, reaching for the bag.

She stared at me in surprise and pulled it away. "What?"

"Oh, sorry." *Hurry, Stella! Come up with an excuse!* "It's just that I'm on trash duty and—"

"Good." Her face relaxed in relief. I'm sure she thought she had a deranged person on her hands. Little did she know. "That can over there is full." She pointed.

"I mean, I dropped something in the trash. I think it was this one. Let me take it and..." I reached for the bag and gave it a jerk, relying on her being caught off guard. It worked. "I'll be right back for the other can in just a minute!" I said, waving.

She gave a lackluster "Okay," as I spun away. Ooomph! Right into a man's chest.

"Excuse me," a deep voice said.

I looked up.

It was the guy in the suit.

19

I jumped like I'd been hit with a stun-gun and whirled away without apologizing. I smiled again at the lady in the white hat and hurried in the direction of the kitchen, the bag thumping against my leg. No doubt she definitely thought I was crazy, after running into someone and not even saying sorry. I was sure she might even follow me. Maybe him, as well. I had to get that letter out fast.

Trying to look like I wasn't running from rabid animals, I scurried into the kitchen. There, I spun around, trying to find a little hiding place. Aha! I spotted a door to a closet or something. I opened it to discover a pantry filled with paper plates, eating utensils, cups, and small cooking appliances. Perfect! I shut it behind me and opened the bag.

My nose wrinkled at the sight of baked beans, macaroni salad, and chicken bones. Then the smell hit me and I actually heaved. Quickly, I shut the bag and my eyes at the same time.

Okay, Stella. You've got to do it. You're tough. You're tough.

Lies! My inner voice yelled. But I ignored it. I am tough. Just hold my breath. Get in there, and get out.

Right then, I heard heavy footsteps. That cinched it for me. I ripped opened the bag, adrenaline making me forget to hold my breath but also fueling me to dig in under the paper plates. I knew the note had to be close to the top, and sure enough, there it was. I plucked it out, gave it a quick shake, and jammed it into my back pocket.

Just in the nick of time. The door swung open. I stared owl-eyed at the man in the suit.

"What are you doing in there?" he asked.

"Oh, I thought this was where the trash was kept." I brushed past him, not eager to remain trapped in the closet. "How silly. It must be over there." I walked to the other side.

He followed after me and grabbed my arm. "I said, what were you really doing in there?"

"Let go of me!" I snapped, jerking my arm away.

"What's going on in here?"

The two of us glanced over at the entrance. Lo and behold, it was Officer Carlson. All nearly seven feet of him. His bald head never looked so good.

The man's hand immediately dropped off of me. "I was going to see if she wanted me to take out the trash."

Officer Carlson glanced at me for confirmation. I nodded and passed over the bag. "Sure," I said, probably sounding as wooden as I felt.

The man stared at the bag and then back at me. He gave me a tight smile and then grabbed the bag. A moment later, he marched out the back door.

Officer Carlson watched him go. "How about it, Hollywood? What was it really?"

I was so relieved to see him, I didn't even care about the tease. I was, however, puzzled if I should yank out the paper in front of him without knowing what was on it myself.

"Well?" he prompted, his eyebrow lifting. His dark eyes shone as he considered me.

I glanced at the back door where I could see the trash container. The man in the suit was nowhere in sight. Slowly, I pulled out the note, wet with garbage juices.

"I was after this," I said, handing it over.

He eyed it a moment before gingerly taking it from me with

two fingers. His muscles flexed as he smoothed it out on the counter. He and I practically bumped heads leaning down to read it.

"Easy, now," he said.

DON'T FORGET. *You're in this as deep as I am.*

"Wow," he said, his eyes locking onto me with curiosity. "What made you go dig this out?"

"I saw that guy who just grabbed my arm read it and then ball it up. You know, the one that followed me in here."

"Yeah, but what cued you in to watch him in the first place?"

"He was talking with Jasmine. It was an odd conversation, ending with both of them upset."

He read the note again and pursed his lips. "Well, congrats, Hollywood. You definitely stumbled onto something interesting here."

"You think so?" My spirits lifted. I'd been disappointed that it had said so little.

"Yeah, I do."

"You going to let me know what you think it means?" I asked.

He touched the side of his nose and then shot his finger towards me. "Maybe I will, maybe I won't. You have yourself a good night, now. Stay out of trouble, you hear?" With that, he sauntered out the back door, possibly to look for the man.

I stood there watching my one clue walk away in the pocket of the most arrogant, irritating man known on the planet. I balled my hands in fists. The stickiness reminded me that they needed to be washed a.s.a.p. I walked to the sink and flipped on the water, as dark thoughts came within a breath of being muttered about how I'd show Carlson that I didn't need him to tell me why the paper was so important. Because I needed some respect!

Immediately, the song filled my head, and I felt the dance moves electrify me. I mentally sang the words, shaking my hips. Shake it to the left! Shake it to the right... Shake it.... My eyes caught my reflection in the microwave window. I looked like an idiot, and what was worse, someone was watching me.

I spun around.

It was Robbie from the gym, standing in the doorway with a goofy grin on his face. "Stella." He nodded, sounding pleased.

"Robbie!" I was more shocked than embarrassed. Then heat filled my cheeks. I wanted to cringe, until I remembered how I'd always tried to be self-controlled. To portray that savvy business woman that my dad wanted so much for me to be. I wasn't what he expected. Heck, half the time, I wasn't what I expected. I was me, and I would learn to embrace that; the good, the bad, and the... weird. This was me, world, take it or leave it. I grinned at Robbie and did another little shimmy and then shrugged. "The music called me."

"Can't deny the music," he agreed. His eyes lit up and he wiggled his hips back.

I giggled, until the reason why we were both here clicked in my head. Ian. "I'm surprised to see you here. Did you know Ian well?"

His smile dropped from his face, replaced by sadness. "Yeah. I used to train him actually. He was a good guy. Died much too young."

"I'm so sorry. I knew him as a client, but he was my uncle's good friend."

"Your uncle did a good job up there on the microphone." He smiled at me, quite an endearing one. And I couldn't help but notice how *well* his suit fit.

"Yeah, I was proud of him," I said, reminding myself not to stare at the way the jacket stretched across his shoulders and his forearms.

"I wanted to tell a story myself, but I guess I'm too much of a chicken." He rubbed his neck and glanced down.

I wanted to immediately wipe that shame-face off of him. "What was it?" I asked. "You can tell me."

"Well," he said, stepping closer. "Ian was really interested in nutrition as well as fitness. It was a good thing, because up until he met me, he thought eating an occasional fast-food salad meant he was eating healthy."

I frowned as that hit a little too close to home.

"Anyway, I got him all set up with vitamins and some protein powder. He was especially interested in supplements and essential oils, so I started teaching him about that, as well. We went to the Heritage Dispensary and got him all set up with a basic kit, you know things to help fight viruses, calming oils, things to help you sleep. He was fascinated with that stuff. Well, I get a phone call that night and he's freaking out. 'What's the matter, Ian?' I asked. He said he thought he may have been coming down with the flu and decided to use the germ fighting oil. Turns out he forgot to use the carrier oil and applied the germ fighting oil straight to his skin." Robbie could barely continue as laughter shot out of him.

I stared at him blankly, waiting for the punchline.

"He wiped it in his armpits! Concentrated oil, not diluted. He said that he ran around like a human goal post with his arms in the air for who knows how long. He could barely put an arm down to make the phone call to me!"

"Oh, it burns, huh?"

"Burns like a mother." Robbie grinned.

"So, what did you do?"

"Aww, I had him wipe it with carrier oil first, and then some soap and water. You have to be careful with that stuff. That was Ian's first lesson. One he never forgot." He shook his head as the smile slowly slipped off his face. "Poor guy."

Poor guy is right. This burning skin story was hitting too close to how Ian had actually died.

But what toxic thing had he gotten into that none of us had? He'd only gone to the kitchen for antacids, and then to the bathroom. Jasmine had even talked to him and he said he was fine. Just washing up.

Was it on the soap? That didn't make sense. I'm sure many people used the bathroom through the course of the party.

"You okay?" Robbie asked.

"What? Uh—yeah. I feel so awful for Ian."

"And his wife," Robbie tacked on.

"Yeah, her as well." It didn't come out with much conviction. She *had* been the last one to see him. And the police did say she stood to inherit a huge insurance policy. As much as I'd been reluctant to accuse the petite blonde, she was coming out as my number one suspect. Still, I couldn't forget Celeste's adamant comment when she said that Jasmine had always been soft and shy, and prone to bullying.

That didn't sound like the makings of a killer to me.

Unless she'd been bullied too far.

20

*R*obbie and I chatted some more until I put the kibosh on it. He'd started hinting with questions about a possible date, first asking me what I was doing next weekend, and then asking me if I liked ice-skating.

I knew one thing right off the bat. Robbie was cute, and I might entertain a date with him sometime, but there was no way I was getting asked at a memorial. Heck no. It can't bode well for a future relationship if it starts over a plate of funeral coleslaw and crockpot meatballs.

So, I gently interrupted him by pulling out my phone and acting surprised that my dad had texted. With a quick promise to see him soon at the gym, I headed out.

I waved at the door, and he cheerfully waved back. Relief

filled me, both at having avoided the close call, and that I'd managed to not hurt his feelings. He seemed satisfied with the promise that we'd talk another time.

The memorial was winding down, with clumps of what seemed to be close friends and family members left. I saw Uncle Chris standing in the same group with Jasmine, both smiling and seeming relaxed.

He caught my eye and lifted his hand. Feeling like I could make my escape, I waved back and then headed out.

As I drove home, I thought about what I'd like to do next. I really wanted to track down the Valentine's gardener. The women's conversation, with all the gossipy bits about Ian and Jasmine, hadn't left my mind. Maybe he could shed some more insight on the Stuber couple. I couldn't help a little smart-aleck grin, imagining calling Officer Carlson and being the one to give *him* the scoop.

But instead of doing something as productive as that, there was another thing I was committed to. Something dark, devious, and horrible. Something I'd love to get out of but I'd never live it down.

Kari's dinner party. Also known as the 'blind date.'

Kari had left me at the memorial with an ambiguous "See you tonight." She was gone before I could respond. I drove home, feeling slightly claustrophobic, as if the mouth of a trap were closing over me.

When I got to my house, I saw that the local hardware store's truck was in my driveway. My flooring had arrived. I needed to call Mrs. Crawford, my landlord about it.

She had made a deal with me that I wouldn't have to pay rent if I didn't mind fixing up the place. It was the most amazing deal ever, and I didn't want to screw it up. It had been slow going, but so far I'd stripped off mountains of wallpaper, patched walls, and painted. There was a cute spot by the stairwell that I framed, that had a poem scrawled in childish handwriting. Mrs. Crawford had done it when she lived here, all those years ago.

So when I saw the original flooring peeling, I'd asked Mrs. Crawford if I could fix it and she okayed the suggestion right away. In fact, she'd asked me for the measurements, which surprised me, because I thought for sure she'd want me to pay for it. And now, here it was being delivered.

It's one thing to say you thought you could lay flooring; it was a completely different story when you saw delivery men bring in box after box—twenty total—and stack them overflowing in the foyer.

The last one was brought in and laid on the heap with a

grunt. I thanked the delivery guys and shut the door to stare, wild-eyed at the pile. *What have I done to myself this time?*

I counted the boxes and quickly checked that there was no damage that I could see, and then rang up Mrs. Crawford.

"Hello, dear," she answered. Her voice was threaded with grace, mirroring the elegant woman that she was.

"Hi, Mrs. Crawford! I just wanted to let you know that the flooring's arrived. I have it stacked in the foyer, and it's all safe and sound."

"Already? They're early. They said they'd be there tomorrow."

"I was a little surprised to see the delivery truck myself. Luckily, I got home in the nick of time."

"Well, that's wonderful. Now, I have faith in you, but tell the truth. Do you think you can handle it?"

The internet... how did people in the past live without it? I'd already spent a few evenings watching flooring videos, and even went to the hardware store and purchased the necessary tools. "I assume there's a bit of a learning curve but I'm up for it. They say it's not too hard."

"That's wonderful. Are you starting on it tonight?"

How I wished I could answer yes. "No, I actually have something else planned for tonight. Maybe this weekend."

"That sounds perfect. Now, why so glum, dear? Oh, that's right, is it the funeral?"

I felt more like I was about to go to a funeral, than returning from one. "No. It's Kari and her husband. They invited me to dinner."

There was a pause. Then, "I'm not quite understanding...." She let the last word dangle with a slightly questioning tone so that I would be forced to fill in the blank. She had skills that way.

"They invited another person. A man."

"I see." And I knew she did see, because she had done the same thing to me not too long ago. "So you aren't seeing David any longer?"

I cringed. David was the man she'd recently introduced me to at a dinner at her house. He'd been very nice, and we had good conversation, but I'd never heard back. No telling who ghosted who in that situation. "No, we haven't had a chance to connect."

"That's too bad. I thought you both hit it off quite well."

People who set other people up *always* thought that.

"Life has been crazy busy. Probably for him as well. Anyway, now I have this new guy to meet."

"Well, it's not going to do any good with that kind of attitude."

I sighed. "I just want to stay home."

"No one's asking you to marry him, Stella. Put your big girl britches on and go out and meet people. Have fun. After all, it often takes a lot of meetings to find the one you click with. My goodness, you'd never believe how many beaus I had before Mr. Crawford. But when I met him, I just knew. Sometimes you have to go through a lot of 'no's' to find out exactly what makes a person a 'yes.'"

"I get it. I just feel like I'm too busy right now to get into a relationship. I have my job I'm trying to figure out. These house projects...."

She laughed. "Stella, if you wait until you have all your ducks in the row, you'll still be waiting while your life passes you by. You've got to be okay to not have everything perfect before you take a chance."

She always had a way of putting things into perspective. We chatted some more about flooring aspects, and then I hung up to go get changed.

Ready or not, socialization was about to commence.

I ARRIVED at Kari's house, where she answered the door beaming with excitement.

"Stella! You look amazing!"

I was a little disheartened by how shocked she sounded. She grabbed my arm and practically dragged me in.

I saw Joe standing a few feet away with another man.

Kari presented him like a proud parent. "So, Stella, *this* is Thomas."

I looked down at him at over five inches. Shorter isn't necessarily bad, but it is when you're wearing your stilettos because your friend forgot to give you a heads up.

"Hi," I smiled, holding out my hand.

He was cute in an average-looking way. Brown hair cut short. Glasses. "Hi, Stella! You're a tall one, aren't you?"

"It's these shoes," I pointed, as if it weren't obvious.

"Come on, let's go sit." Like an energetic teenager, Kari directed us to the couch. I awkwardly sat, my skirt rising.

"Ohh, you're wearing that skirt! I love it!" Kari said.

I shot daggers at her and smiled through clenched teeth. She was wearing jeans and a comfy blouse. "Thank you."

Thomas checked me out a little. "Yeah, I'd say on a scale from one to ten, you're a nine."

I felt a little rebuffed. "Thank you?"

He grinned and leaned back on the couch. "And I'm the one you lack."

The first 'Nope' of the night resounded like a gong.

Kari caught the expression on my face. "All right, Thomas, leave your jokes for later." She brought us over a glass of wine. A pendant hung out of her shirt, swinging as she leaned over.

It caught my attention immediately. "Kari, what is that?"

"Oh, this?" She slid a thumb under the chain and brought the pendant closer. "Isn't it cute?"

It looked like a little filigree tube. "It's adorable. What is it?"

"It's my aromatherapy vial. This one is for creativity. I needed all I could get when the oven broke."

"The oven's broken?"

"Yes! And it was a two for one, since Joe forgot to fill the propane tank. So no steak tonight. Instead, we're having tacos!"

I didn't care about that, so caught up in the vial. "That's great. So how does it work?"

"See," She unscrewed the lid and showed a tiny stopper. "I just put a little dab on. Smell it." She thrust it under my nose, forcing me to smell it whether I wanted to or not. I took a sniff. It was pleasant. But I didn't care about the smell, I was so interested in the top.

"Kari! That top is similar to what I found in the bathroom. That piece of jewelry, remember?"

Her mouth dropped into an O. "I can't imagine Jasmine would own anything like this I mean, it's not cheap, but it's no designer piece."

"I don't know. She seemed like she was into oils."

Kari shrugged. "Like I said, it doesn't seem quite her style. Or Celeste's either. Maybe it belonged to one of the caterer's."

"Maybe." I wrinkled my nose, thinking. "By the way, what did you think of your last conversation with Celeste?"

"She seemed uncomfortable, didn't she? Of course, small town Brookfield is hardly her stomping grounds. Not quite yachty enough." She raised her eyebrow and gave me a look.

"I remember you said that. Jasmine seems like the exact opposite."

"Yes, quite the homebody, I think. She didn't want to move, you know. Actually, she suggested that they keep two houses, and have Ian move to the city alone."

"When did she do that?" I asked.

"When Ian was signing the listing agreement. Jasmine said it was her dream house and she loved it. But Ian wouldn't hear anything she had to say. He definitely ran that show."

"I heard she was kind of rescued by him. Maybe that's why Jasmine felt like she couldn't say anything. Maybe he threw it in her face."

"Well, you know what they say. When you marry for money, you earn every cent of it."

That was such a depressing statement. I nodded.

Joe didn't seem as impressed. "Hey, we going to eat or what? Gossip later because I'm starving!"

DINNER WAS A SUCCESS. How could any meal that consisted of tacos not be a success? The wine continued to flow, emboldening Thomas to declare at one point, "You are the guacamole to my burrito."

I had to laugh. Kari soundlessly mouthed "sorry," to me and

Joe got out a card game. By the third round, we were all laughing, and I was actually quite pleased I'd decided to come after all. Thomas must have figured out he was friend-zoned, because, although he did walk me out to the car that night, he merely said, "I had a lot of fun. But the next time we play cards, it's going to be for real money."

21

Sunday morning woke me with a beam of sunlight cutting straight through the minuscule space between the curtains to land right into my face. I groaned and pulled the pillow over my head. Forget flooring, I need to get blinds on that, stat!

Still, it was a good idea to get up. I wasn't used to drinking wine, and who knows how long I would have slept in. I sat and cupped my pounding head and remembered why I didn't drink wine.

Never. Again.

I groaned some more and floundered out of the covers and into the bathroom like a cross between a zombie and a catfish.

By the time I had my shower and brushed my teeth, I felt much more human.

And it was a good thing because I had a list of things I wanted to do today. Needed to do, actually. First on my agenda was to see if I could talk with the gardener, the one that the Valentines hired. I remember Charity mentioned that he came on Sundays, and from what she'd said, he had a pretty good scoop about the Stubers. One that seemed to agree with the argument that the Clark's had overheard.

The second thing on my agenda was to visit the Heritage Dispensary to check out their pendants. I wasn't sure how useful it would be, but it would be interesting to see if I could identify the vial by the top I'd found, if I could remember it correctly. I wish I'd taken a picture of it before handing it over to Officer Carlson. Who knows, maybe they even had a record of who bought it, especially with their classes and such. You never know.

After starting my coffee maker, I pulled up the MLS and searched for houses that had sold on Novelty Hill in the last year. It didn't take long to find the Valentines' new place. It was literally a stone's throw away from Jasmine's home.

I really, really didn't want to get caught at the Valentine's house though. I could only imagine the glee in Ms. Valentine's eye as she called the cops on me for trespassing.

So I decided to do some snooping instead. There, I said it. I was a snoop. But only when I needed to, I reminded myself.

An hour later found me driving past Jasmine's house. I couldn't help staring as I went past. The house blinds were down, with no cars in the driveway. Maybe they were parked in the garage.

I stepped on the gas when I realized I'd slowed down way too much. *Be cool, Stella!* Geez, watch me get reported to the police on me on my first stake-out. I could just imagine Officer Carlson with his wry grin and funny dimple coming to haul me away.

Wait a minute... a stake out... was that what I was doing? I shook my head. No, it was nothing that sinister. I was just on the lookout for a company gardening truck that Charity had said would be there today.

Beautiful house after beautiful house went by. Finally, I spotted a rose hedge, likely part of the rose garden that Charity had mentioned.

As I approached, I caught sight of something so shocking it made me gasp. And not a sweet gasp, more like sucking in on a tin whistle. Quickly, I jerked the car to the side of the road and slammed my brakes.

No, no, no. It can't be.

Parked in front of the Valentine's house was a black truck.

My jaw opened like I was a seal trying to catch a fish. I just couldn't believe it. In fact, was I even sure? I mean there had to be a million black trucks out there.

Oh. Yep.

There was the silver frame around the license plate. That's it. I wasn't going to mess around. I fumbled for my phone to call Officer Carlson.

Then I paused. What would he say? Probably one of two things. Why didn't you report this black truck at the time? Or option B—You do realize that vehicles often turn around in roads and it probably had nothing to do with you.

Maybe I could just get a little closer and see who the driver was.

I parked my car and, after glancing both ways to see if anyone was watching, climbed out. Feeling about as stealthy as Velma, I tiptoed over to the very healthy and very green hedges. Cautiously, I parted two prickly branches to peek through to the house.

The house was cute and quiet. But no one was in sight.

I was considering my next move when I felt a tickle on my head. Annoyed, I swatted at it. I swear it moved down my neck.

Now I'm a squirrelly kind of gal when it comes to bugs. You get me around a spider, and I'm more dangerous than any ninja. The problem is that I've freaked out too many times over nothing, so I knew exactly how my imagination worked. It even happened at the surprise party when I had sweat trickling while hiding behind the couch. My brain starts exaggerating little tickle sensations—see, there it goes again, it feels like it's down my shirt. Right now, I was on a serious stake-out. I definitely couldn't afford to let my imagination run away from me this time.

Besides, this was getting ridiculous. My brain was imagining that it had gone down my pants. And everyone knows that bugs do not crawl down pants.

I stood there, feeling the tickle argue back with my logic. Finally, I gave in and hurried back to my car. I was going to look like an idiot in the please-don't-let-there-be-a cop-drive-by-and-arrest-me-for-indecent exposure kind of way, but I had to check. I climbed into the back seat where at least there were tinted windows and lowered my pants.

A big, fat beetle waved one crawfish leg at me. I screamed so loudly, I'm positive the windows rattled.

"Ew! Ew! Ew!" But how to get rid of him? I couldn't very well flick him free in my car, and I couldn't open the door until my pants were in their proper place.

First things first. I grabbed a napkin and whisked him onto the floor and then shimmied back into my pants, mentally cursing myself for ever second-guessing a creepy crawly feeling.

Then I carefully lay down the napkin and hoped the beetle will crawl on it.

He was not having it. Not after being swept away from his warm home so rudely. No, his beetly little brain seemed to decide that he was going to strike out on his own. He started to lurch under the driver's seat.

"Oh, no you don't," I said, thwarting his march with an old fast food bag. I heard whistling up ahead and glanced up.

Coming around the hedge towards the black truck was the guy in the suit that I'd seen at the funeral. The one who had chased me down when I was carrying the garbage.

My jaw dropped open as I stared.

Today, he was dressed more casually, but still wore a sports jacket. He opened the truck door and stepped up onto the silver running board. Then, for some reason, he paused and glanced back in my direction. Nightmare of all nightmares! I ducked, hoping I wasn't noticeable in the back seat.

I froze, waiting for the sound of the truck door closing, my breath hot against my knees. The beetle waved a leg at me from the floor as if warding me off from getting too close.

What was *he* doing here? Why at the Valentines' house?

The whistling stopped. Now my heart speeded up. What was he doing? Was he coming closer? Did he recognize the vehicle? I hyperventilated, afraid to move, held hostage by a bug.

Finally, the truck door slammed. I heard the engine turn over and then the gravely sound of tires grabbing the road. I chanced a peek just in time to see him speed away.

I sat up and watched him disappear around the corner, my mouth feeling as dry as an abandoned corn husk. I realized I was going to have to risk Ms. Valentine calling the cops because I had to know who he was. And the only way to find out was to go ring their doorbell.

But first, it was time to say goodbye to my little friend. Between the bag and the napkin, I managed to scoot him onto the paper and then shake him outside on the sidewalk.

"Sorry, buddy," I whispered as he waddled rather indignantly into the grass.

Feeling like a hot mess, I smoothed back my hair and took a deep breath. *I've got this.* Shoulders back, I walked up the driveway of the cute, Bavarian-inspired cottage.

It was easy to see the ladies' attraction to this home, with its old charm construction, sweeping overhead trees, and fragrant rose hedges.

At the porch steps, I took a few more breaths, like I was the quarterback about to run the football through a defensive line. Then I marched up the stairs and knocked on the front door.

There was a patter of footsteps, a clatter of a lock being turned, and then it swung open to reveal Charity. I caught a glimpse in the window of my face set in a grim, determined line and reminded myself to smile.

"Why, Stella! You found us!" The tiny woman clapped her hands. She'd always been eager to have a reason to celebrate.

Thumps echoing through the dark interior heralded the approach of her tall sister. Soon, Ms. Valentine was at the door. She didn't say anything, just arched a brow suspiciously at me.

"Look, Sister, it's Stella!"

"I see that," she sniffed. "What can we do for you? Do you want to try and get another Valentine arrested?"

Oh, boy. This was not going well, and every sense in my body was telling me to get off that porch and fast. Instead, I pushed through.

It was at that startling moment that I realized I needed to come up with an explanation of why I was standing there, like a student peddling cookies for summer camp. My brained whirred, flashing different lies in my head, each one I promptly rejected. A lost puppy— no. Car broken down—no. Lost—good grief, Stella. *No.*

Finally, a suitable one popped up. "I was driving through when I noticed that gentlemen leave in a black truck. I used to know someone who had a truck like that and wondered if it could be him. I happened to see he left this house, and much to my surprise, it's you guys."

"Guys? We're not guys," Ms. Valentine dragged out the last word, staring down her nose.

"Ladies," I apologetically amended.

"Oh, that was Jeffry," Charity offered, oblivious to the nudge her sister gave her. "He's our gardener."

That was the gardener? The shock must have shown on my face because Charity continued. "Jeffry owns the business. He does all of our yards. He dropped by to say that he was retiring soon, and would be hiring someone to take over our place." She sighed and batted her eyes. "I'm going to miss him."

"What about your boyfriend at the nursing home?" Ms. Valentine asked, dryly. "Love is fickle, as they say."

"I can look, just not touch," Charity pouted. "Anyway, I hope he finds someone who will take care of our lovely Sunsprites and Lincolns as well as he does. He does have such an eye for roses. Since we hired him, he's really had a vision of bringing this garden back to life. He's even saved some heritage roses I haven't seen since my childhood!"

"Fancy they're still around, Charity. You would have thought they'd died out with the dinosaurs."

"Oh, pooh," Charity said. "You're older than me, you know."

Ms. Valentine said nothing but rolled those pale eyes. I smiled, loving the more relaxed nature of their relationship now that the burden of the old Valentine manor no longer rested on their shoulders.

"How did you find him?" I asked. "Your gardener."

"He came highly recommended. The whole neighborhood uses him. He's famous for using natural things to fight fungus, mildew, and bugs. It's quite amazing."

"We're all green around here," Ms. Valentine commented, slightly ironic.

"Really? Like what?" Charity's zeal was reminding me of something. I struggled to remember it.

"Oh, different things. Once it was soap bubbles. Beautiful smelling, it was."

I thanked the sisters for their time and then headed back to my car. As I passed the hedge, I couldn't help whispering goodbye to the black beetle, wherever he was.

Back in the car, I pulled out my phone. It was time to figure out who Jeffry was.

22

*I*t's a funny thing. It seems you can't type in "Jeffry the gardener" and expect any serious links on a search engine. I clicked on a few—and click out just as fast on one that made my jaw drop—before I realized that wasn't going to work.

All right. I'll bite the bullet and put a call in to Officer Carlson. Of course, he wasn't there. I asked to be patched into his voicemail.

His request to leave a message was as dry and grumpy as I imagined it would be. Finally, it beeped, and I said, "Officer Carlson, I found out that the jewelry is a piece of a roller ball for an oil vial. It's probably from Heritage Dispensary. I'll check later and let you know. And I forgot to tell you, but I had a weird thing happen with a truck that I thought was following me. Well, guess who owns the truck? The guy that had that note at the funeral. Well, I'll talk to you later so...."

I hung up. Most awkward goodbye ever.

Shaking my head at my suaveness, I searched up the address for Heritage Dispensary and started the car. Carefully, I turned around in the Valentines' drive and backed out onto the road, then started back to town. So Jeffry, huh. He was the gardener that spread the rumors about the Stubers. What was this all about?

I was still deep in thought when a white Hummer flew out of a driveway. I screamed and slammed on the brakes. The car narrowly avoided t-boning me and, without slowing down, sharply turned onto the road.

I gasped for air, trembling like ice-water flooded my veins as the Hummer sped away. What had just happened? I turned to look. The vehicle had come from the Stubers' house. I tried to swallow, realizing Jasmine almost killed me.

I was trembling too much to drive. I had to calm down. I pulled into the Stubers' driveway, sending up a few thanks for still being safe and sound.

It was ironic, sitting in Jasmine's driveway after nearly being run over by her. I took a few cleansing breaths and stared down the driveway. This house was the start of it all.

Something Ian wanted to get away from, and a place where Jasmine wanted to start a family.

But how much did she really want to start a family when she suggested that he leave without her? That doesn't make it sound like a very happy home. I studied the meticulous landscaping, the arched doorway and the enormous window perfect for displaying a Christmas tree. This house looked like it should be full of love. Instead, it was full of ... what? And yet, Ian's death made Jasmine happy because now she was able to stay. Marla Springfield's words rang in my head. Some places aren't right. Home strange home.

As I was sitting there, the front door opened. I straightened in the seat. A feather could have knocked me over when I saw Jasmine step out onto the porch. She stared in my direction, her eyes squinting to see. Her brow lifted and she smiled, waving a hand.

"Stella! What are you doing here?"

If words were Scrabble pieces, I was left with a box of vowels with no consonants. I was so gobsmacked, all I could think of were sounds of, "Ahhh, eeeeh, uhhh."

She continued down the pathway, and I saw she was in her slippers. I hurried to get out. There was a moment of panic when I couldn't unfasten my seatbelt—it had locked when I slammed on my brakes— which added even further to my conundrum.

"H-hi, Jasmine," I said when I was finally free and standing outside the car.

"Was there something I forgot to sign?" She smiled pleasantly up at me.

"Uh, no." I rubbed the back of my neck, not sure if I should tell her that one of her guests nearly ran me over like a Mac truck. Her eyebrows lifted questioningly, and I realized I wasn't in the frame of mind to form an acceptable excuse. I was forced to tell the truth.

"Who drives the Hummer? Because they flew out of here like a bullet and nearly took me out. I actually pulled in here to try and calm myself down." I held out my hand, which was still trembling from the final effects of the adrenaline burst.

"Oh, my gosh! Are you okay?"

I reassured her I was.

"That was Celeste," Jasmine answered. "She's always been a crazy driver. Come in. Let me get you something to calm you down."

I followed her inside, not at all certain about what she was going to offer me. It turned out to be a glass of water. "I'm sorry, I don't have anything else. I'm even out of coffee!"

I sipped the water. "How about you, Jasmine. How are you doing? I know yesterday must have been rough."

"I'm doing okay, actually. Your uncle did an amazing job at the memorial. And Celeste is staying here to keep an eye on me. She normally travels a bit, but she dropped everything to make sure I was okay. I'll get through this." She smiled then. It was a tough smile, and for a moment, I caught a glint of a waitress who had the fortitude to fight off her manager.

"I'm glad Celeste is able to stay with you."

"She's amazing. She'd do anything for me." Jasmine glanced around her house. "You know, this was my dream house. As horrible as everything is, I'm glad I get to stay here."

Her comment weirded me out a bit. Still, I knew grief affects people in strange ways. "It's probably a comfort to be at home at a time like this."

"It is. This place is my life. I never wanted to move. That was all Ian. Still, I would have. Kicking and screaming, I would have. He's done a lot for me, so I owed him. It's amazing how sometimes situations feel like a prison sentence."

I caught on to something there. Now, my intuition normally was about fifty-fifty. But this was so obvious no one could miss it.

Something had been very wrong in their marriage. It was too much to piece together, and to be in this house, where he died—where he was murdered—it felt too icky to try and sort through.

"Well, just take it easy on yourself while you figure things out. It's a strange time," I said.

She held up her water glass as though it had wine. "Cheers to that."

I LEFT her house a few minutes later, buckled myself in, and headed back to my second goal on my agenda. The Heritage Dispensary.

On my way there, I thought about the conversation the Clarks had said that they'd overheard. It was then that Jasmine had first mentioned serving a life-sentence. She'd also mentioned she thought she was pregnant. And Ian had denied it, saying he'd had a vasectomy.

I narrowed my eyes. If she'd meant that marriage was a life sentence, then it had dissolved pretty quick with an actual end of a life.

And how was the gardener involved? Jeffry. The Valentine's said that he gardened for the Stubers as well. That he was there a lot. Charity said everyone loved him. He didn't seem all that lovable when I met him.

Still puzzling over all of this, I drove through town in search of the address I'd found.

A few moments later, I located it. Sunday was a quiet day in town so parking was plentiful. I parked the car and walked over.

Immediately, disappointment hit me. The lights in the business were off and, as I walked closer, I saw a closed sign in the window. I sighed and started to turn back to the car when it occurred to me the sign was swinging. Just a tiny bit, but it made me hopeful that maybe the person was still in there.

I knocked on the door and then peered in the window. There was no one visible. I was about to give up when something prompted me to try the door handle.

It clicked under my hand, and the door swung open.

"Hello?" I called.

No answer.

There was music going.

"Anyone here?" I asked again.

The place inside was set up almost like a book store, and the scents... wow. Although it was dark inside, I smiled to see a shelf filled with books up on the support beam overhead. There was a sign that said, "Books for tall people."

That was refreshing. It was nice to see a place that was professional but still maintained its sense of humor.

That was it... that's what struck me about how Charity was describing the gardener's natural alternatives, her voice was filled with devoted zeal.

I heard a small crash like someone had dropped a book onto a table. "Is someone here?"

It was then that I saw it. A foot. Someone was lying down behind the counter. "Are you okay?" I yelled, running over.

What I found made me cover my mouth in horror. There was a woman on the floor. She stared up with frightened eyes, tape over her mouth and her hands tied. She shook her head, her words muffled behind the tape. I leaned over and tried to ease a corner off.

"I'm here to help. I'm calling the police right now."

"Run," she whispered.

At that moment, the front door slammed behind me.

23

My head jerked up at the sound as I held my breath to listen. The dark room only had a bit of light filtering in around the crowded displays in the windows. Below me, the woman's eyes were wide, and she started to struggle. I waved my hand to try and silence her muffled cries.

Could it have been a draft that caused the door to shut? I didn't hear anything more, but I was too scared to peek over the top of the counter. I tipped my ear.

Nothing.

And then a tap. Tap. Tap. Silence again.

The music played loudly. I mentally cursed at the person who had left it on. I couldn't hear anything more.

I scurried to the end of the counter. Cautiously, I peeked around the corner, searching for feet. Specifically, high heels.

That was the clinking noise I'd heard, I was sure. The tap of a heel on the floor, its sound only made by a very thin stiletto.

There was nobody there.

I eyed the front door which seemed a galaxy away. I needed to get over there, but how? Was it safe? Had she left?

Slowly, I eased my way back past the poor woman on the floor. With my hands, I indicated that I was going to call for help. I crept down the length of the counter and peeked around the other end.

It was clear.

There were aisles in front of me, set up like a book store. If I could get in there, I wouldn't be as trapped. Right now, hiding behind this counter, I was like a bug caught under a cup.

Could the woman stalking me see in this dim light? I was having a hard time, so my guess was that she did as well. My muscles tensed, readying me to spring forward.

"I couldn't find the receipt, so I destroyed the computers." A man's voice. It came from the back room.

I jerked down at the sound.

"Shh," cautioned the woman. The stillness that followed

pressed heavily on me as if it were a physical thing. The shallow gasps I was taking weren't sufficient. I gasped faster, feeling like I couldn't breathe.

"What's going on?" he asked.

"Seems like we might have a mouse," she said. There was a sharp, metallic click. I recognized the voice.

Celeste.

I recognized the click as well. Someone had pulled the hammer back on a pistol.

My heart thudded harder than it ever had before. If I didn't get out from behind here, I would be boxed in. I searched in the gloom for something, anything, that might help.

"What do you want me to do?" asked the man, moving closer.

Under the counter was a shelf of bottles. At his voice, I grabbed one and threw it hard down the counter in the opposite direction from myself. Then I ran.

My target was the door in the back of the room. I raced for it, praying I'd get past the man. He was standing to the left and I felt the wind of his hands grabbing for me as I flew past him.

"Get out of the way!" Celeste screamed.

The gun went off. I nearly collapsed at the sound, sure that

I'd been hit. My legs never stopped, propelling me forward and through the door.

I had two seconds on the other side to decide which direction I was going to go. There was no brightly lit exit sign like I had hoped. Instead, it was set up like a mini warehouse, complete with rows of metal shelving. And nearly pitch black, the only light coming from a single bulb in the office where the radio was. I darted to the left and raced down a few rows, looking for a place to hide. I just needed time to call 911.

Time was running away.

I ducked behind a box to listen. Did I hear the door open just now? I covered my mouth and nose, trying to stop my gasping. My lungs heaved for air.

I heard a sound to my right and spun to look. Celeste's silhouette darted behind a shelf. How did she get over there?

It was then that I realized she must have removed her shoes. The thought of her tip-toeing on bare feet, unheard, brought a cold sweat. I couldn't risk being heard either and carefully slipped off mine.

The laminate floor was cold under my feet. Ice cold. It seeped through my socks and into the pads of my heels and toes, where it met epinephrine-fueled blood.

I didn't dare search my purse for my phone. I couldn't risk

making a sound. I peered through the shelving, searching for her. It was too dark to see much of anything.

Quietly, I moved to the end of the aisle. I peeked around. There it was! Finally! The exit sign.

A shadowy figure passed under it. I ducked. Were they both in here with me? I doubted it. I couldn't hear anything, and I didn't think the man would be so silent.

Which hardly helped me in the situation with a gun.

The aisles were set up as straight chutes toward the back of the building. Once I chose an aisle to run for the exit, there was nothing for it but to race to the end. And I couldn't outrun a bullet.

What had happened to that poor woman? Was the man out there with her? Would he hurt her?

I forced myself to forget about her. My escaping was her only chance, and mine as well. I needed to focus. Gritting my teeth, I struggled to fight back the fear.

Where was Celeste, now? My thighs trembled from my crouched position. I could barely stand the pain. I moved to ease my weight when my shoulder brushed what must have been a trash can. The plastic bin scraped several inches across the cement floor.

Did she hear that over the music?

I had to do it now. Had to make the phone call whether she could hear me or not. There was no more time. Slowly, I eased my phone out of my purse. My heart pounded so hard I could hear rushing in my ears. Adrenaline had kicked in again and now was on overdrive. I typed in my password, flinching as my shaking fingers hit the wrong numbers.

I tried again and my phone locked once more. Frustration filled me. This was a living anxiety dream.

Calm down. Focus. I typed one more time.

"Stella..." Celeste said, nearly in my ear. I jerked. She was on the other side of the shelf. I hadn't heard her approach. "Let's talk. Come out. I'm not going to hurt you."

I hid the phone against my chest, trying to shield the light. Did she see it? She had to have. Breathing out slowly, I eased down the other end of the aisle.

"911. What's your emergency?"

Crap! I threw the phone but not before the gun went off. BANG. I screamed and punched my hands over my ears. Uncontrollable tremors overtook my legs.

Get up, Stella. Get up, now.

I rolled to my hands and knees and started to crawl. I could hear Celeste now. She was headed in the direction I threw the phone. I rounded the corner and past several more aisles.

"Jeffry!" Celeste screamed. "Jeffry get in here and help me!"

I saw the exit sign and ran as fast as I could. As if hell hounds were at my feet. I had to get down this aisle before they saw me.

I know they heard me.

"Over here, Jeffry!" Celeste called, her voice closer now.

My socks slipped on the laminate, and I nearly fell. I grabbed the shelf, knocking bottles and boxes to the floor with a horrific clatter.

The gun went off again. I was so close. Almost there.

"Stop her, Jeffry!" she screamed.

Heavy footfalls came behind me. Feet moving faster because the shoes had purchase against the floor.

Every bit of my track knowledge came to play. Muscle memory ignited, and I had another burst of speed.

Just seconds to the door.

My hand grazed the doorknob. Relief flooded me, quickly dashed as a hand grabbed me by the back of my shirt.

"Got you," his hoarse voice whispered in my ear.

Not so fast. I spun around and struck out with the heel of my hand, connecting with his nose. He shouted, cursing. I didn't look to see what damage I had done. As his hand loosened on my shirt I was already turning back and twisting the knob.

Bright light blinded me. I stumbled through, already searching for which way to go.

A voice froze me in my tracks. "Get to the ground, Hollywood!"

2 4

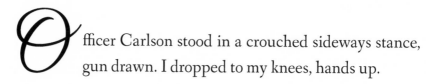

Officer Carlson stood in a crouched sideways stance, gun drawn. I dropped to my knees, hands up.

The skin on my back crawled. I was dead center in front of the open doorway. What was happening? Was he going to force me to surrender while Celeste shot me from her hiding place inside?

His gaze was intense, and I realized then, that he wasn't staring at me. He was staring right into the storehouse. He skirted around me until he was at the side of the entrance.

"Stella, move from the doorway," he commanded quietly.

I eagerly did, half crawling, half rolling until I was out of the way.

When I looked back, Carlson had disappeared inside.

So he knew the bad guy was still inside? How had he found me? Did they trace the 911 call? I climbed to my feet, ready to run. I wasn't sure what to do next. Did he need help?

I hesitated, wondering if I should run for a phone.

"Police! Get down!" Carlson screamed. There was a sound of boxes falling and metal clattering.

"Jeffry!" Celeste shrieked.

And then...silence.

My heart pounded. What if they came running through that door? They're going to run smack into me! That thought ignited my feet to move. I found a dumpster and crouched behind it.

The cold air had a greasy scent of old French fries, and I shivered. The silence was nearly intolerable. What was going on in there?

A second later, gunshots split the air. I screamed. Who had shot the gun? Celeste? Carlson? My worst fears played in my mind of Officer Carlson in there, bleeding, while the two of them came out to hunt for me. Hot tears burned my eyes at my complete helplessness to do anything about it.

That's it, I'm running for help. It took every last ounce of courage I had to get up and be once again in line of sight of the door. I stared at the opening, like a wild animal, and edged along the building wall until I was at the corner. Then I ran like my life depended on it.

Or Officer Carlson's.

The first door I tried was locked. "Closed on Sundays," it said in cheery letters.

"Please! No!" I cried, beating the door. I darted away to the next one, which had also closed early for the day.

I couldn't believe this. My breath was coming in hot pumps as I ran as fast as I could. I'd tried to flag down a car, but they raced away, honking at me. Was there no one to help?

Finally, I spied the giant doughnut slowly spinning. Darcy's Doughnuts. I raced over there and ripped the door open. It bounced back against its hinges and everyone inside stared at me, some in mid-bite.

"Please!" I gasped, out of breath. "Please! Someone call 911. There's been a shooting at the Heritage Dispensary. The gunman is still inside!"

No one moved.

"Please! He could be dying!" I begged.

That spurred some action. A mother sitting at the table with her two young children quickly dialed. In nervous stuttering, she relayed what I said, eventually, handing the phone over to me.

"They want to talk with you," she whispered, staring at me as though she were afraid it was me that was the wild gunman.

I took her phone. "Please. Everything she said is true. And Officer Carlson is inside. He went in after them, and a gun went off. He might have been shot."

Most of the doughnut shops patrons were at the window, straining to see if they could spot something. The mother called her children away.

"Stay on the line please," said the operator.

I nodded, before realizing she couldn't see me. "I'll try. This isn't my phone. I'm at Darcy's Doughnuts right now."

"Stay on the line," she warned.

The mother overheard and reached over to pull out a chair. I sank down, gratefully. Someone else came over with a cup of coffee. I even had a glazed doughnut passed my way.

But I couldn't think of anything but help coming. "Are they on their way?" I begged the operator.

"They're en-route. Stay put."

I didn't know how much more 'put' I could stay. I was antsy like I'd just finished a carafe of espresso.

"There it is!" someone called.

I listened. Tears sprung into my eyes at the sweet sound of sirens. "They're here. I can hear them. Thank God!"

"That's good. Stay with me," the operator said calmly.

We watched the cars flash by. One. Two. They kept coming. Five. Six. Then an ambulance raced after them, making my heart leap into my throat. I turned away from the window, feeling queasy. *Please let that cop be okay.*

25

*O*fficer Carlson gave me a little wave as I hurried over to the Heritage Dispensary. I was jumbled in among a crowd of onlookers, and the police had their hands full trying to keep us away. It's amazing he even saw me. Of course, it's possible that when I saw him, the relief was so strong that I screamed his name.

One second later, I was embarrassed, but not by much. I was deeply grateful the guy didn't die running in after some bad guys that had shot at me.

He did get shot though. Two paramedics helped him up on the stretcher while he tried to shoo them away. His legs were too long for the thing and his feet hung over like boat anchors.

Once he was settled, he waved me over. "Daniels! Let her through. She's a witness."

His partner cleared a path for me to get past the barricades. When I finally reached the stretcher, a paramedic was trying to put a blanket around Carlson's shoulders. He pushed it away with a scowl.

"Are you okay?" I asked, trying to see his injury. His left arm was bound and held in a sling.

"Just a flesh wound." He shrugged nonchalantly.

"They say that in real life? I thought that was only in cheesy adventure flicks."

"You would know, Hollywood."

"Where are...?" I glanced around for Celeste and Jeffry.

"Those two are over there." He jerked his head in the direction of two more ambulances. "They'll be slowed down for a while. At least for their trial. Fired on me, so they got what they deserved."

"Well, they fired on me too," I said, and then cringed, realizing I sounded like I was one-upping him.

"Yeah. And you got away. That's impressive." His dark eyes studied me. Did I detect a sparkle of respect in them?

"Why were you there?" I asked. "Did you guys track down my phone call?"

"Track down your... girl, you really do watch a lot of movies, don't you? No, I did this thing called deducing. It's kind of part of my job."

"How did you know I was going to be at the Heritage Dispensary?" I was impressed with those deduction skills of his. He was smarter than I'd given him credit for.

He rolled his eyes. "You told me. Remember. 'Hey, I'm going to go to the dispensary and check out the jewelry stuff.' I was on my way to see what you dug up. I heard gunshots, and then you burst out the door like you'd been blown out of a cannon. Now you know what I know."

"Are they going to be okay?" I dipped a shoulder toward the other ambulances.

"Yeah, but you should be more worried about the owner."

"I am! Is she okay? Where is she?" I stood on tiptoes, searching.

"She's talking to Detective Simpson over there. She has quite a story."

My head swiveled back to him. "What happened? What did she say?"

"That there is Mrs. Lavender."

I narrowed my eyes at him.

He held up his hand. "That's her name. Scout's honor. She's the manager here at the dispensary. Jeffry came in all masked up and tied her up. Then he let Celeste in."

"What was she looking for?"

"She was looking for a credit card transaction. Specifically for one roller ball necklace with a top like you found. They destroyed the computer in the back room, which wasn't smart. The bank has all the transaction information. And Mrs. Lavender is prepared to testify."

"That Celeste bought the necklace? And killed Ian Stuber with a topical oil."

Now it was his turn to narrow his eyes. "Yeah. How did you know?"

"I didn't know, not really. I suspected, but I wasn't sure. But seeing her tonight obviously was the hammer to make the last piece fit in the puzzle."

"You use a hammer when you're putting together puzzles? Geez, that's harsh."

Obviously, he was hurting too much to be nice. I remembered something else. "Did you get their phones?"

"Officer Daniels has them. So you think those two were a couple?"

I shook my head. "No. Celeste wasn't in love with Jeffry. Jasmine was."

He raised his eyebrows. "Really? And how did you come up with that?"

"You see, it started with the fact that Ian was never home. Celeste felt the need to inform me of that when I first met her. She didn't like him much."

"Later, I found out that Jeffry was their gardener, and everyone in the neighborhood liked him. He spent a lot of time at Jasmine's place. They were lovers."

"Keep it coming, Hollywood. I like this movie you're spinning."

I ignored him. He was probably delirious from pain. "His truck showed up outside my house right after I'd asked Jasmine about the necklace. I knew he was a local because my neighbor recognized him as well. She just couldn't remember his name. And later when I saw Marla Springfield, she said people had been talking in the restaurant about how I needed to butt my nose out of other's businesses. We need to ask her but I'm willing to bet one of those people was Jeffry."

"So, all that has to do with Jasmine. Why is Celeste involved?"

"Jasmine was weak. Celeste said it herself. Jasmine never stood up for herself. She didn't want to go to New York with Ian. She wanted to stay at her house and with Jeffry. But she wouldn't get a divorce. In fact, she told Ian that she was pregnant. Ian insisted it couldn't possibly be his. That proved to me that she really was weak like Celeste said, resigned to stay in a marriage that she herself termed "a prison sentence," even going so far as to pass a baby off on Ian that wasn't his."

"Ian knew about Jeffry. I bet he was probably planning his own revenge himself. Marla Springfield, from the diner, told me that she overheard a horrid conversation between Gordon and Ian. Gordon was explicit that he could send the gardener back in a box if he gave Ian any more trouble. From what I hear, Gordon's got connections."

"Yes, he does. Go on." Officer Carlson gruffly pressed.

"So, Celeste saw herself as Jasmine's protector. It wasn't hard. She already hated Ian, and it probably seemed like a simple solution that, in killing him, Jasmine would be free to live in her house and be free to be with Jeffry. After all, Celeste told me herself that she always helped Jasmine with bullies.

The plan was simple. Celeste knew Ian had indigestion. She took classes on essential oils and knew how to use the right carrier oil. She had Jasmine giving him supplements and oils to help."

"Those are made to help."

"Right, so to make it toxic, Celeste had to get a hold of a poison. Something so vile, it would kill nearly instantly. But that it would look like a heart attack. She must have talked it over with Jeffry. That's when he told her that he had smuggled back mushroom's from China. Specifically, Little White's."

I waited to see if that would sink in. Officer Carlson had the amazing gift of keeping his expressions locked tight behind a stone face. He was giving me that stony look now, although it did appear a tad annoyed.

Hurriedly, I continued. "So the day that Ian died, he used one of the oils on his neck. It was in a roller ball. He must have collapsed nearly instantly, losing the cap. Celeste got rid of the bottle, but couldn't find the other piece."

"So Jasmine is innocent."

"I think she might be. Both Celeste and Jeffry killed Ian for Jasmine. One out of family loyalty, and one maybe out of love. Poor thing. Now Jasmine has nothing left but her home."

"That's a big story. Could be a bunch of hot air, you know," he said.

I shrugged. I might have some details wrong, but my gut feeling told me I was pretty close.

Officer Carlson didn't get a chance to respond. The paramedics came in and gently nudged me to one side.

"Come on, Champ. Time to get that bullet out," One of them said, as they wheeled the stretcher to the back of the ambulance. Officer Carlson grimaced as they collapsed the front legs and loaded him into the ambulance with a bump.

I peeked inside. "Get better soon!"

"We'll talk later!" He gave me a cute grin and they shut the doors.

Wait. Did I just think that? Gah!

Shaking it off, I went over to the police officer guarding the store entrance to see about getting my shoes back.

2 6

The next day, my phone rang off the hook with calls from news reporters. I wanted to keep my name out of the media as much as possible, and after a few "no comments," I put my phone on silent.

I did need to get ready though. Uncle Chris had sent a message asking for a Flamingo Realty meeting for lunch. He wanted to meet at a small pub, but I talked him into moving the meeting to Springfield Diner. Kari was right. Their bacon burger was to die for.

And I had worked up an appetite. I'd spent a good hour that morning talking with Dad. He was less than reassured about the events from the night before, even when I told him I was fine. I may have down-played the actual gunfire a bit, so he wouldn't worry. Our call ended with him still dubious about my move to Pennsylvania and a few bribes to try and get me to move back. When I was adamant about staying here, he'd sighed and said he was going to look into a plane ticket to visit me soon.

Honestly, my heart was singing after I'd hung up with him. He was finally, finally coming out after all these years. My hope of getting the family back together was *this* close. I could feel it.

Quickly, I finished getting ready, and then grabbed my purse and keys. After skirting around the flooring boxes—good grief, what *had* I gotten myself into?—I jogged out to the car.

As I was backing out, my phone dinged with a text. I checked it really quick in case it was Uncle Chris.

It was from Officer Carlson—**Have a second? Call me.**

I hit dial and put the call through the car's speakers. "How are you?" I asked, when he answered.

"Getting out of here today."

"Oh, that's great!"

"Yeah, like I said, it was just a nick. Anyway, first things first. We tracked down the phone call that Ian was on during the surprise party. Two guesses on who it was, and I'll tell you right now, it wasn't his brother."

"It was Jeffry."

He growled. "How did you know? Do we have a leak?"

I shook my head. "It had to be him. Ian said he'd kill him. Very few emotions cause that kind of hatred to come through a person's voice, but talking to someone your spouse is cheating on you with will do it every time."

"And you don't wonder what the extortion part was?"

"What was it?"

"Jeffry wanted money to leave Jasmine alone. Otherwise, he was going to follow them to New York City."

"How do you know that?"

"Celeste and Jeffry gave a full confession. In fact, Celeste said, and I quote, 'I just wanted Jasmine to live her best life. Sometimes people need a little nudge to get there.' Jeffry's wasn't so saintly, and had more to do with money, sadly."

"What about the note I found at the funeral?"

"It was from Celeste to Jeffry, to remind him to watch his p's and q's. He was getting a little antsy when Ian's death got ruled a murder. The Little White poison he'd used was supposed to mimic a heart attack. He never suspected it would be identified as the cause of death. He was freaking out because he'd bragged to more than a few people when he got back from China that he'd smuggled in the mushroom, and was afraid someone would put it together."

I smiled. *Say it, Officer Carlson. Someone like me.*

He wouldn't though, and I wouldn't bring it up either. After all, if I hadn't renewed my license on the day I had, and run into the Valentines, I never would have learned that information. "Wow, so it's over then."

"It's over. Now I don't want to be hearing from you for a long time. At least about something like this. If something else comes up, maybe we'll talk."

I laughed, and we hung up. As I turned onto Main Street, I did puzzle for a second over what he meant by his last line.

Yellow police tape distracted me. Down at the corner, Heritage Dispensary was still closed with the investigation. A shiver ran through me, remembering the events of yesterday. It felt like a lifetime ago. I did want to go in there when life had mellowed out. I'd like a chance to introduce myself to Mrs. Lavender under better circumstances.

The red-and-white awning of the Springfield Diner cheered me up considerably, though, and with visions of a bacon burger in mind, I parked and walked into the restaurant. It only took me a second to spot Uncle Chris sitting at a round table near the window. Kari wasn't there yet, apparently.

Well, I wasn't waiting for her before I ordered. I walked back there, smiling.

He looked up and saw me and I watched his face crumple into five different emotions. First, his eyes widened—fear. He swallowed and clenched his fists, and then he smiled, tight-lipped and fake.

I won't lie, my steps faltered. Fear? Why would he look afraid at seeing me?

I swung my purse off my shoulder as I approached. "Hey, Uncle Chris," I said, keeping my voice easy.

"Hi, Stella." He stood up and waited until I sat, before sitting back down himself. He cleared his throat and took a drink from something he'd already been served from the bar.

"Gin and tonic," he said, wiping his lip. "You want one?"

"It's a little early for that, don't you think?" I asked. Alarms were ringing in my head.

"Hi, you little trouble maker," Marla said with a smile. I glanced up, having not heard her approach. "You've got to keep a better eye on her," she admonished Uncle Chris.

He grinned, a weak one, and nodded. What was up with him?

Marla turned back to me. "So did you ever thank that hot rod guy?"

Hot rod guy? I felt like I was caught in someone else's conversation. "What do you mean?"

"When you were in here the other night." Her dark eyes twinkled. "He must have seen you through the window there and parked that fancy car of his to pay for your dinner. Said that you looked like you'd had a hard day. Didn't Tammy tell you?"

With so much else going on, I'd completely forgotten about my dinner being paid for by a mystery man. "Who was he?"

"Well, that was Richie Wilson. He owns Wilson Mechanics up the road. Moved most of his business out to his mom's place, but he does good work. Yeah, he loves them hot rods. Just bought that purple Challenger the dealership had for sale. Boys and their toys."

Uncle Chris nodded at me. "And girls too. She wanted that car."

"Did you, now?" Marla nodded, studying me. "I think you better be thanking Richie then. Sounds like someone you should get to know." She winked.

I half-heartedly smiled back. Since I'd entered the restaurant, I couldn't shake the feeling that I was on unstable ground.

We gave Marla our order. It was weird. Uncle Chris hemmed and hawed like he was reluctant for her to go. So when the silence descended between us after she left, I wasn't surprised.

He sighed deeply, as though his very soul were groaning.

I slowly shook my head. My hands squeezed together under the table.

"Kari's not coming. I needed to talk with you," he murmured.

My jaw clenched. There'd been a point when I'd wanted to hear what he had to say, but now I wasn't so sure. My life was finally getting stable, getting back to a place where I'd wanted to be for a long, long time.

And I knew. I knew that what he had to say was going to blow all that up. My stomach rolled over in revolt. Everything I'd worked so hard for these last few months hung in the balance like the bead of sweat on his upper lip.

"Please..." I said, shaking my head.

"Stella," he answered. "I've needed to have this talk with you for a long, long time. I've been afraid."

"Uncle Chris, I don't need to know anything. I'm fine just where we are. You don't need to talk with me about anything, especially if it makes you afraid. I—"

"Stella!" His voice was stern as he cut me off. But his red-rimmed eyes belied the sternness. He took another sip. "You sure you don't want a drink, Stella?"

I shook my head.

"You're going to need it," he said. He waved his arm to beckon the waitress. She walked over with a smile, not realizing a disaster was about to happen.

"What can I get you?" she asked, setting a glass of water before me.

"Another gin and tonic for me. And for her—"

"Nothing," I muttered, feeling sick.

"She'd like a shot of brandy."

"My, my," she said, her eyebrows lifting with admiration. She walked away.

"Uncle Chris—" I started.

"Wait," he said. "Wait until she brings the brandy."

"I'm not going to drink it," I answered, crossing my arms. "I'm not sure what this is about. If you're so determined, you should just spill it."

He waved a finger at me and stared desperately after the waitress. A moment later, she walked back with the two glasses on a tray. He watched her approach like a man watching the prison trolley roll in with his last meal.

"Here you go," the waitress said, setting the drinks down. "Can I get you something else?"

"Maybe later." He quickly took the last swig before handing her the empty glass. Then he clutched the new drink with both hands.

I stared at my shot glass before me, the fumes of the alcohol rising up. Then I raised my gaze to meet his. This time I didn't say anything. I just waited.

"Stella, I knew your mom."

I nodded. I suspected he did. What was so startling about that? Then my eyes widened. What was he going to say next?

"I know where she is."

I swallowed, fear freezing me from speaking.

"You're not going to like it. You're going to be very angry with me. It's the real reason your dad left all those years ago. And I'm sorry, honey. You're going to hate your grandfather, Oscar as well."

"Why?" I whispered.

Because he's the one that took her from us. From you."

Slowly, he unveiled a story I never wanted to hear. Each word tore my family away. My father. My uncle. Oscar. My mother. When he was finished, I was left orphaned, abandoned, and betrayed. And I never wanted to see any of them again. I jerked back from the table, the chair scraping harshly against the floor, and I ran out of the restaurant with Uncle Chris calling helplessly after me.

I DROVE AWAY from the restaurant in a sweat, in a panic. I don't remember how the conversation ended, or where I was going. All that was running through my mind was Uncle Chris's face and this horrible, gut-wrenching feeling of loss and betrayal. My mother was alive, but in prison, most likely for life. She'd been a Pit Lizzard, a Nascar groupie that hung around at the race track. My uncle had met her first. They'd only been friends—or so he claimed. I didn't know what to believe anymore. But he admitted, his face pasty white as he spoke, that he'd gotten her addicted to drugs.

Later, she fell in love with my dad. Dad had helped her clean up her life, and they had a little family. She had me. And then my uncle lured her back to one more party.

I don't know all the details. I couldn't care less at this point. I know it had something to do with a drug dealer that Oscar had been investigating. What mattered was that something horrific went down, and my mother had been sent to prison for murder.

Oscar had taken her away.

I needed to talk to someone, but who? My friends from back home never heard me talk about my mom. They wouldn't understand. Kari had a life of her own, and honestly knew Uncle Chris better than me. I could never go to her.

And Oscar....hot tears coursed down my face. How many times had he comforted me, pretended he'd cared, when, all along, he'd known what he'd done.

The rain lashed against the windshield. Three men in my life stole something from me. My father stole the memory of my mother. My uncle set the temptation in place to draw her away. And my Grandfather put her in prison.

Lightening flashed outside, echoing my heart. The black clouds couldn't match the dark thoughts in my head. I could barely see, and who knows if it was the rain or the tears.

I found myself standing in the downpour at the foot of Mrs. Crawford's wide veranda. I'd gotten out of the car, and trudged straight through the mud puddles that had formed at the sudden dump of water, not caring.

My nose ran, but there was nothing left to dry it with. I stumbled up the stairs and stood, shivering, on the welcome mat. I had no idea what she'd think. I usually only came by her house to pay my rent, and what with the deal we made, she'd know that's not why I was here.

She opened the door without a smile, having seen me through the glass.

"Stella?" she said. "Is something wrong at the house?"

I shook my head. "It's fine. It's just... please, I'm sorry for barging in." I didn't even know what I was going to say to her. "I just had to be around someone right now."

"Absolutely. Let me get you a towel." She scurried back down the hall and came back a moment later with a white towel. Hummming comfortingly, she wrapped it around my shoulders, bringing a scent of lavender. Its heavy weight was welcome, and I wiped my face on the corner.

"Is it Oscar?"

I nodded. "He's not dead or anything." The words came out grudgingly. My life felt changed forever.

"Come on. Let's go sit down and talk a spell." She led me into her sunroom and sat me on the settee. She settled into a white wicker chair across from me and nodded, and her kind face made me burst into tears again.

"It's my uncle. He told me the worst story. All the men in my family have betrayed me."

And, for the first time ever, I cried over the loss of my mom. Everything spilled out. She nodded and hmmed sympathetically through the whole ordeal, though I have no idea how she understood me through my hiccups and rabbit trails. She didn't ask any questions, just gave me space to let it all pour out like the rain from the clouds.

When I was done, she stood up and tucked the towel a bit more around my neck. And then she disappeared into the kitchen where I heard the sound of water running and the comforting clinks of stoneware. A moment later, she came back with two steaming mugs, one of these she settled into my hands.

I took a sip and stared at her a little nervously, waiting to hear her response. But instead, she leaned back to relax and nodded at me to do the same. We sipped our tea and allowed the soft sounds of the rain to fill the silence for a while. The downpour had turned into patters that lightly danced across the ground.

When she did speak, her voice was low, comforting. "Stella, I hear your frustration and pain at the consequences that other peoples choices have caused in your life. Your anger, your grief, and your feelings of betrayal are all understandable.

But you need to know you *are* going to get through this. Even though now you might not be able to see how, this is not where you will always be." She took a sip of her tea and watched out the window. "You know, sometimes I think our greatest fear in life is that the situation we're in right now is forever. I can tell you from experience, you won't always feel the way you do today.

You have a beautiful story... the story of your life. Take the time you need to sit here in your emotions and then wipe your face. Your story doesn't end here. You will figure out the next step. As my father always said, 'Look up. There's always a path ahead.'"

I nodded. I couldn't think too much past the anger right now, but I knew in my heart that Mrs. Crawford was right. Life was different now. I didn't know all the ways that it had changed. But I knew one thing. When I looked up, all I saw was a path leading to my mother.

THE END

THANK you for reading Home Strange Home. The story continues in Duplex Double Trouble.

Here are a few more series to whet your appetite!

Baker Street Mysteries— Where Oscar and Kari are first introduced! Join Georgie, amateur sleuth and historical tour guide on her spooky, crazy adventures. As a fun bonus there's free recipes included!

Cherry Pie or Die

Cookies and Scream

Crème Brûlée or Slay

Drizzle of Death

Slash in the Pan

OCEANSIDE HOTEL COZY MYSTERIES—MAISIE runs a 5 star hotel and thought she'd seen everything. Little did she know. From haunted pirate tales to Hollywood red carpet events, she has a lot to keep her busy.

Booked For Murder

Deadly Reservation

Final Check Out

Fatal Vacancy

Suite Casualty

ANGEL LAKE COZY MYSTERIES—ELISE comes home to her home town to lick her wounds after a nasty divorce. Together, with her best friend Lavina, they cook up some crazy mysteries.

The Sweet Taste of Murder

The Bitter Taste of Betrayal

The Sour Taste of Suspicion

The Honeyed Taste of Deception

The Tempting Taste of Danger

The Frosty Taste of Scandal

AND HERE IS Circus Cozy Mysteries— Meet Trixie, the World's Smallest Lady Godiva. She may be small but she's learning she has a lion's heart.

Cirque de Slay

Big Top Treachery